Praise for Presumption

In his debut novel, Fisher paints a compelling western romance imbued with intense passion, friendship, tragedy, and violence rooted in racial bigotry. Both the characters and plot are vividly realized. I can't recommend *Presumption* highly enough.

~ Jane Alvey Harris,
author of *Riven* and *Secret Keeper*, winners of Literary Classics International Book awards, Book Excellence awards, and National Indie Excellence awards.

In *Presumption*, Hank Fisher has woven a ravishing epos of internal and external landscapes. The rugged realm of the old West stands in exquisite contrast to the sensibilities of Darik, the Romanian birdhouse-carver, searching for love against the tribulations of frontier reality. Fisher has built an inhabitable world of authentic historical fiction, one you can gallop along in until you feel yourself in the saddle of yearning and destiny. If lightning strikes, horses, corrupt bandits, and harsh terrain light your fire, the heart of Fisher's immigrant wanderer will throw the first spark on the tinder of your imagination. *Presumption* is a tender, wild ride.

~ James Scott Smith,
author of award-winning *Water, Rocks and Trees*, *The Expanse of All Things*, and *Wild God of the World*.

Hank Fisher weaves a story which threads together a sense
of history, a love of the natural world in its sensory detail,
and a reverence for the creativity and desire for connection
with source that is the engine of human nature. This is
a contemporary fable written with a poetic eye and a
dreamer's spirit.

~ Devika Brendon, Senior Content Editor of the literary
journal, *New Ceylon Writing*; Consultant Editor for the
SEALA Global Network; and internationally published
poet and author of short stories.

Presumption

Presumption

Hank Fisher

ISBN 13: 978-1-944662-70-7

Publishing date: October 2021

Front cover Photo by Hank Fisher

Cover Design by MASGraphics © 2021

Dedication

To my wonderful mother, Helen, a gifted artist who didn't begin her serious explorations into painting until the final two decades of her life, but who poured compassionate creativity and boundless love into every breath she ever took.

And to my father, Mort, the most down-to-earth philosopher and brilliant businessman I've ever known who once told me, "Don't worry, you've got a novel or two in you just waiting to be written once you apply your unfiltered views of life to your writing."

Thanks to you both!

Acknowledgments

When I set out five years ago to write Presumption, my debut novel, I gave little thought to how many retirees (from their professional careers) had embarked successfully in crafting and publishing his or her first novel as they approached their seventy-first birthday. It just never occurred to me. Not ever.

I've written more than two dozen revisions during these past five-plus years, countless tweaks, lots of rethinking, a few attempts at re-sequencing events and timelines, and invoking subtle personality alterations on my various characters, not to mention finding the right voice for the first person, third person, and overarching narrative sections. I've put the manuscript away a few times since day one in 2016, several quiet periods lasting two to six months each so I could work on new poetry for my next chapbook or two--plus so I could determine how best to approach working through the challenges and bliss of writing a novel and what I wanted to do with it if and/or when I ever completed it (at times I wondered if it would occur).

Now that Realization Press, under the leadership of Drew Becker (thank you, Pam, for the referral), has completed its end of the process and published the e-book and soft cover versions, I want to express my thanks to several tremendously creative and considerate ass-busting professionals who stepped up to the plate when I sought their input and whose commentary and suggestions were all taken to heart (almost always, but not quite always—for after all, I'm a handful to deal with).

Thanks to my first editor, Dawn Peterson, whom I began working with after the second iteration of the manuscript was completed in 2016. You cannot imagine how helpful your comments and suggestions were as I delved into my intent, re-examined certain elements of the storyline, sought ways to improve character development, and looked at what needed to be done to transform the story into a novel.

Much gratitude to Jane Alvey Harris, a two-time National Book of the Year winner for her first two novels, *Riven* and *Secret Keeper*, for providing me with great insights about the strengths and deficiencies of an early version of the manuscript, and about the need to clarify my characters' points of view, and generally in helping me elevate my storytelling into a finished manuscript that others might want to read with publication of the novel. Your input was crucial as I refined my manuscript.

Big thanks to Melissa McKinstry, a gifted educator and poet in San Diego for conducting a beta reading of what was either revision 12 or 13; I've lost track. Your perspectives were necessary for me to confront in terms of character development and areas where the plotline might have gone astray or needed tightening up. I listened carefully to your input, and after I let the manuscript marinate for a few months, I dove back in and tried my best to incorporate your responses and suggestions.

To my fantastic editor, Diana Henderson, thank you a thousand times over! I'm so grateful you took me on as a client and managed to help fine tune the manuscript in everything from minor structural corrections to rethinking dialogue and the internal thoughts of primary characters and to tidying up things in ways that I rarely disagreed with because you know your stuff, big time! As I've gotten older, I've found myself enjoying the editing, proofing, revising, and tweaking of my writing, be it this novel or the volumes of poetry I've composed. Working with you as a partner during this crucial stage of the project was delightful and educational. What helped considerably for a debut novelist like me was being able to understand and embrace your commentary and suggestions, and then implement your recommendations. Your positivity from start to finish was fantastic.

To my kids, David and Rachel, for helping guide me into the realm of fatherhood beginning four decades ago and even without realizing it, to always motivate me to create and write more, to tell stories, to compete and be positive, and to demonstrate that while time might seem to be 'of the essence' as we move through life—the real key to the journey is not yielding to or being distracted by the real life challenges and obstacles that we either create for ourselves or allow ourselves to be drawn into.

And the biggest thanks of all goes to one of the best writers and most generous and loving individuals I've ever known, my life partner, Dr. Anita Johnston, renown for your best-selling book, *Eating In The Light Of The Moon*, now printed in a half-dozen languages around the world. I owe a debt of thanks to you that surpasses this acknowledgement page, so rather than simply rambling, I'll just keep cooking dinners while you work with your clients, complete your next book, conduct your speaking gigs and workshops around the country and overseas, and tend to the online program (www.LightoftheMooncafé.com) you developed with Elisabeth Cross Peterson a number of years ago that's benefitted thousands of women worldwide since the site went live. I marvel at your frequency, your writing technique and outlook, your incisive knack for finding a 'better phrase' or 'better word' or being able to rip apart (with a knowing smile) your writing projects and starting over in order to improve your article, blog, chapter, or a piece for marketing communications. Your non-stop support blends perfectly with your tough love as my in-house editor. Your presence in my life keeps me energized, productive, and optimistic.

And finally, thanks to Realization Press for transforming my manuscript into a book. I hope I wasn't too difficult to work with, but, at the end of the day, we got it done!

Thanks to all,
Hank Fisher

Contents

Dedication ix

Acknowledgments xi

CHAPTER 1
Thunderbolt..3

CHAPTER 2
Deliverance...5

CHAPTER 3
Revival...11

CHAPTER 4
Recollection..21

CHAPTER 5
Kindred...29

CHAPTER 6
Sendoff...33

CHAPTER 7
Reappearance..37

CHAPTER 8
Harken..41

CHAPTER 9
Enchantment..43

CHAPTER 10
Reconsideration 67

CHAPTER 11
Inferno 77

CHAPTER 12
Exodus..81

CHAPTER 13
Revival..89

CHAPTER 14
Succubus 101

CHAPTER 15
Phantasm 107

CHAPTER 16
Odyssey...119

CHAPTER 17
Serendipity..131

CHAPTER 18
Consciousness..141

CHAPTER 19
Resurrection..157

CHAPTER 20
Fraternity 167

CHAPTER 21
Encounter 183

CHAPTER 22
Heartfelt 197

CHAPTER 23
Recapture 209

CHAPTER 24
Outrage 217

CHAPTER 25
Foreboding 221

CHAPTER 26
Forthcoming 241

CHAPTER 27
Culmination 245

Author Bio 257

JUNE 1883

CHAPTER 1
Thunderbolt

Darik was already a mile east of Castle Rock on Friday morning. It was just after sunrise. Low hanging clouds spinning in opposite directions blew in and settled directly overhead as thunder echoed.

Clementine, the aging pinto pulling the buckboard, seemed uncharacteristically jumpy and hesitated for a moment as the roar of thunder increased. Darik thought something was wrong and wondered if she sensed coyotes or rattlesnakes nearby. He leaned forward and spoke softly to her, making a gentle clicking sound with his mouth while yanking the reins firmly a couple of times. The horse then began to move slowly on the trail toward Kiowa.

The violence of the sudden explosion was massive. The smell of burning wood engulfed the air. The last thing he was aware of as the buckboard blew apart into hundreds of pieces was the brief, terrified sound from Clementine as a lightning bolt struck the center of her neck and Darik found himself in mid-air, thrown back fifteen feet, jolted into unconsciousness before hitting the ground. He found himself adrift in a powerful dreamscape as confusing as most of the others he had experienced since he was a boy.

He was flying over a snow-covered wheat field with the grace and speed of a soaring white falcon pursuing a prairie dog. Small bolts of lightning moved from cloud to cloud, illuminating them from the inside out. He could see through the frosty white powder covering the ground and into the small tunnels beneath the soil where the creatures traveled. His twists and turns through the air were precise. His arms were positioned angularly in the shape of wings stretching outward from the side of his rib cage. He raised his eyes toward the horizon and saw a large oasis an acre in size with a small pond in the center surrounded by sand-covered mounds and a dozen tents, each with a gold amulet hanging in front of the entrance. A young black-haired woman with bronze-colored skin stood alone. A single moonbeam with the intensity of a lighthouse beacon formed a perfectly shaped ring of light with her in the center. He became motionless as his flight suddenly stopped, yet he did not fall from the sky. He felt calm and secure as though he were resting safely on a perch. The woman looked upward into his eyes and whispered something in a loving tone in a language he did not recognize. Then she vanished into a wispy fog, and the oasis was transformed into the interior of a small shop.

CHAPTER 2
Deliverance

Strong winds raked Darik's body as the smoky black cloud hovering over what remained of the flaming buckboard, doused by torrential rains, was transformed into billowy white steam within seconds. He lay unconscious atop a small yucca, bleeding profusely from several spiked needles piercing his back. In those initial moments while rain pounded down on his face, thunder roared, and cloud-to-cloud lightning bolts crisscrossed the sky, he was transported to a familiar place from his childhood, a beautiful farm in Romania where he saw the smiling faces of his grandparents, now deceased for six months although he did not yet know it.

He saw the image of his most cherished possession, a small hide-covered trunk his grandfather made for him as a going away gift when he emigrated to America at age thirteen, a trunk that now held the wood carving tools the old crone in his Romanian village had made decades earlier and that were eventually presented to Darik by his grandfather so he could pursue his carving skills.

According to his grandfather, the wise woman in their village supervised the forging of these tools twenty-five years earlier just before Darik's second birthday. Working with the village blacksmith, the old woman applied her knowledge of alchemy and the spiritual world to help create the sharpest and strongest carving tools possible, ones she knew would one day be used by Darik, a young man who would be blessed with the skills and artistic passion of a master carver.

His mind continued to jump erratically from one dreamscape into another as he lay near death from the lightning strike. He was encased in a warm, all-consuming darkness he would never be able to describe nor remember, but in his thoughts he managed to catch a glimpse of the sunlit silhouette of a young Chinese woman standing alone in a field of sunflowers, a field he could not identify but that seemed familiar.

The details of time had lost their definition as he floated within this vision that made him feel he was on a ship in moderately heavy waters similar to what he experienced on his journey from Romania to America, but he could not remember why this beautiful woman was holding one of his unfinished birdhouses in her hands. It was as though the image of the woman had superimposed itself over his thoughts about the carving tools and his grandfather. This blended vision continued to emerge from the darkness of his mind as she appeared briefly and then vanished, eclipsed by a fluttering darkness.

His mind, groggy and disconnected from his physical body in a way he had never experienced previously, raced between the sharp carving tools and the beautiful face of this young woman while at the same time he could see his hands shaping the birdhouse's interior from a large block of cottonwood, efficiently carving the wood from the inside out by following the technique his grandfather had taught him.

He began visualizing the forty handmade tools in his trunk, each designed for a specific carving function. Some were as tiny as the implements of a watchmaker, while others, including several of the chisels and scoops, were more typical of the finishing tools of a carpenter. He possessed a connection to these tools, an intimate knowledge of their function. He understood them as though they communicated with him directly, much like his mystical connection with trees in the forest and the wooden blocks he carved so proficiently.

Ten minutes passed before the storm vanished as rapidly as it had arrived. Darik, unconscious, his arms and hands charred to the color of coffee in places, his pants and shirt reduced to scorched shards of cloth, was now lying in the bed of a buckboard headed toward Castle Rock as fast as the bumpy road and driver's skills would allow.

The driver, a scruffy-looking woman more than a dozen years his senior, a large ranch-strong woman who owned the apothecary in Castle Rock, realized this young man was on the precipice between the realm of the living and the dead.

Moments earlier, from several hundred feet away, she had watched in horror as rapidly spinning marbled clouds dropped from the sky and a long, narrow lightning bolt took aim on the horse, buckboard, and young man.

When she arrived and saw how little was left of the burning buckboard and horse, she was surprised that the young man was still breathing, albeit barely, as he lay atop yucca needles in what remained of his scorched clothing. She removed his smoldering jacket and lifted him into her small wagon as carefully as possible, covered him with a large red and white checkerboard picnic blanket she kept folded in a small box in the cargo bin, and raced against time to get him to her place a mile and a half to the east.

* * *

"Who's the kid?" the sheriff asked as he and the woman stood over Darik, still unconscious several hours later, but not fatally wounded as she had first thought.

"No clue. No way to know. Buckboard was destroyed. Horse's hide burned so crisp there's no way to see a brand. The boy had papers in his jacket but they're nothing but ashes. It's a mystery who he is as much as it's a miracle he's breathing."

Eighteen hours passed as Darik continued to sleep, trapped in a fog that both nurtured and haunted him. Parts of it were nightmarish distortions of a long forgotten fairy tale that the old crone in his Romanian village recited to him years earlier. She had advised him repeatedly during his childhood to never fear the unknown, even death itself, and had said that within the dark places he might be detoured into during his lifetime, places where death waited patiently, there would also be undreamed of opportunities revealing themselves if he faced the fear and passed through them on his journeys to and from the other side.

Hank Fisher

Free falling from the top branches of a giant spruce, knowing he was headed into the rocky surface below, he began flapping his arms as though he was a bird, a soaring white falcon, and suddenly he was headed upward into a bank of billowy cumulus clouds from which he did not exit.

CHAPTER 3
Revival

Friday morning, shortly after sunrise, a strong and familiar smell of burning sage awakened him from deep sleep.

With his head cocked slightly to one side, he saw the smile of an older woman through his squinted eyes. Her arms were muscular, her weathered facial features far from beautiful, yet her hands looked as soft as those of a baby. The handful of sage was emitting a small, aromatic cloud that brought a slight smile to his face. He could see a mirror-like reflection of himself on the surface of her crystal clear, emerald green eyes. He also noticed that the odors of the sage blended with the pungent smell of some sort of medicine to create a fragrance nearly identical to Woodcock ointment concocted long ago by the old woman in his village.

"Am I dead?" he asked.

"Youngster, it'd ruin my reputation if you croaked so easily. Hell, it was only one bolt of lightning. Not like typhoid fever or a gunshot," she said sarcastically. "Nope. Not sure how you managed to fight off the lightning, but you did. Not as lucky as your horse and the buckboard. Nothing was left of either except a big bonfire of horseflesh and lumber that stunk to high heaven."

"I remember the thunder. That's about it. Something exploded," he said as he edged closer to full consciousness.

"You, that's what exploded. You, the horse, and the rig. Lightning came down out of nowhere and struck the buckboard and horse like someone had taken aim with a buffalo rifle. Never seen nothin' like it. Truly a miracle you're alive. Someone raised themselves one hell of a strong young man. I'm Lynetta. Who are you?"

"Darik, Darik Jacoby. But I can't remember *her* name," he said haltingly, his face depicting confusion. "*She* was in my dreams…. I thought I'd never see *her* again."

"Chasing some young gal, are you? Breaking someone's heart? In love and don't remember her name? Ain't that something. Don't worry, it'll come back to you," she said with a smile. "Surprised you remember your own name after the lightning. Where you from? Interesting accent but you don't sound Irish or Italian, that's for sure, and don't look Mexican or Chinese neither," she added grinning at him.

"Romania. A farming village near Bucharest. It's a beautiful area. Have you heard of it?"

"I'm not school educated, but I read a bit and love looking at maps. I know it's in Europe. You got family there?"

"Grandfather and Grandmother were still alive when I left for America. I don't know anymore. That was thirteen years ago. He was a huge man, taller than me, and I'm a little over six feet. His face was weathered from all the years he worked his fields. He had a cropped gray beard that my grandmother trimmed every Sunday morning. He was strong as a bull, thick and tall like an oak tree, and the gentlest person I've ever known. He was fifty-one when I last saw him," Darik said. The pain was almost too intense for him to speak, but he found that conversation distracted him from it at least a bit. As long as he kept talking, he could push the seared flesh into the background a little longer.

"Grandmother was about the same age. She was tiny, not more than five feet. She had beautiful silver hair, no dark hair at all, at least not by the time I was old enough to notice, and she kept it tied up in a small bundle on the top of her head. Despite her size, she ruled the house. An iron fist and a beautiful smile. Great combination."

Lynetta smiled.

"Neither were school educated. I'm not either," he continued, "but the wise woman in our village was very smart. She was our doctor and wrote letters to me for a few years after I came to Colorado, but it's been two years since her last one. I don't know if she's still alive, but if she is, she'd be pretty old. I learned a little English from her. There was something mysterious about her that wasn't like anyone I've ever met. She had this look in her eyes kind of like you do, and she was always telling stories, some she made up out of thin air. And it seemed like she was mixing up potions and oils all the time, and she could see into the future as though she knew exactly what was going to happen. I'm not making that up. Not guesses either. She seemed to know. Do you believe in that sort of thing? Seeing the future?"

"Must be that you and I were supposed to meet. Sounds like my kind of woman. Maybe she's kin to me," Lynetta said with a knowing smile.

Despite numerous bursts of pain shooting through every part of his body, especially in his burned hands and fingers, Darik managed a small smile as he drifted in and out of consciousness.

He saw another figure enter the room carrying a tray, a young woman closer to his own age. Her golden blonde hair was tied into a woven pattern. There were no bangs or loose strands.

Her hazel-colored eyes offset her pale complexion. On the tray was a large bowl of steaming soup giving off a pleasant aroma. Nonetheless, each beat of his heart brought with it fragmented memories of the lightning strike and varying degrees of pain that caused him to twitch involuntarily.

"Set it down, Ingrid," the older woman directed, "right there on the nightstand. We'll help him sit up and he can try sipping it. From the look on his face, he's doing a good job fighting the pain, but this young man has definitely not won that battle just yet. At least those steely blue eyes are nearly back to normal, a hell of a lot more life in them than when I brought him here."

And with that, the enormously strong woman placed her arms around Darik's upper body and lifted him to an upright position, careful not to touch the burns on his arms now covered by a golden-green salve she mixed in the kitchen the night before.

"What is this?" he asked as Lynetta put a spoonful of the hot liquid into his mouth.

"Cactus soup. It's a potion I make from the saguaro cactus and *Aloe vera* that grow in the basin a little southeast of here. I learned it from an old Indian medicine man who began riding through here years ago. Hell, it's been at least fifteen years since he's been back. We became friends the first day we met, and I became his student I guess you'd say. He taught me everything he could about the flowers and plants growing in these parts and swore to me that the Utes, his tribe, as well as the Kiowa and, hell, even the Arapahoe and Pawnee, had been using this cactus mixture for healing up cuts, burns, and snake bites for centuries. And from what I've seen over the years I've lived here, he was damn right. Not bad tasting neither."

"Reminds me of home," he said as a soft glow began to fill his face. "Yep, reminds me of home. Good. Thanks. I was hungry. Feels like I haven't eaten in a month. Could I have some water?"

"All you want, youngster," Lynetta replied. "Mineral water if you don't mind. I think it's delicious, but I'll warn you it's kind of an acquired taste. It's from a small underground channel that runs behind my store, maybe a hundred feet from the back door. That's one of the reasons I settled right here. Once I tasted this magical water for the first time I knew it had special healing powers. I truly believe there's enough natural goodness in this plateau to heal an army after a battle. And the hot spring's a godsend. I love soaking in it. I'll show it to you sometime. Once you're all healed up, maybe you'll come back here and give it a try. It's truly amazing."

He nodded. "Forests. I grew up near forests. Grandfather and that old woman back home, they taught me to listen to what the trees and plants have to say. And I'm good at it. The trees might have tried to warn me about the storm, but sometimes I forget to listen. Sometimes I forget that the trees and me have a connection. Most people I've met don't believe in talking to nor listening to trees, but it's real. Most people think I'm crazy when they hear me talk about nature and trees the way I do, so I just keep quiet about it. But I can tell you understand that there's a world of knowledge in all that grows.

"I carve birdhouses," he said with an abrupt change of subject, or so she thought. "I carve them out of solid blocks of wood. Not just any wood, only wood that speaks to me and gives me permission to create birdhouses from it. Seriously, I can hear the wood and it's always seemed like the wood reads my mind. It's a blessing, I guess, a favor the wood offers to me as long as I treat it and all forms of nature with respect and do my best to make beautiful carvings. And there are these small openings, narrow little slits that I carve into the sides of each birdhouse. Each one makes a special sound, kind of a chirping song when any wind blows over it."

"Birdhouses? You carve birdhouses? Ain't that something," Lynetta said in a puzzled tone. "Out of solid wood? Can't imagine. Must be damned difficult? That's your job?"

Having taken the spoon from Lynetta, he sipped more of the cactus broth and shook his head as exhaustion overtook him as though a blanket had been pulled over his torso. "No, not really… just something I've always done. I'm a ranch hand at Eagle Trail Ranch near Littleton. Mostly do carpentry. I fix things there, you know, odd jobs. I'm good at it too. I'm supposed to pick up a few horses in Kiowa and bring them back to Eagle Trail. Silvano, foreman of the ranch, will kill me when he finds out I lost the pinto and buckboard."

At that moment, every detail of his last conversation with Silvano flooded his mind. "Oh god," he said in a worried tone as Lynetta watched silently, "He'll go through the roof. He'll probably fire me. Oh crap!" he said as his final conversation with the ranch's foreman came back to him as vivid as the moment it occurred.

"Darik!" he remembered a voice shouting, "you gotta take the buckboard to Kiowa tomorrow! First thing at sunrise. Want you out of here by sunrise. Got it? No later. Boss bought three ponies from the Firmans over at Double Canyon Ranch. Bring 'em back. Alive. And you need to deliver that bitchy chestnut mare in the far corral to the livery in Louviers on the way out."

"Who's going with me?" he asked.

"You! Just you! Too busy here to have anyone else leave the spread. Boss likes you for some fucking reason I don't understand. You know I don't like you much," the man said laughing. "Me and the Hebrews have never gotten along very well. Same thing with the Orientals. If I wasn't a mixed blooded Mexican, I wouldn't like Mexicans neither! Boss said to send you on your own. Trusts you more than anyone else but me even though you're just a foreigner from someplace nobody's ever heard of. Four days round trip. Not five. Four. You been to both places with me. When was the last time? Last autumn? So you gotta know the route by now. Jews any good at directions? Don't want you getting lost in the desert for forty years. Get there and back without pissing me off."

Silvano, born and raised in Oaxaca, Mexico, chuckled. "And no stopping for pussy at the Louviers' whorehouse. You know every one of those gals on a first name basis, at least the names they tell you are real. I hope you don't believe a fucking word they tell you. They'd say anything to get the money out of your pocket, so keep your chaps and boots on for the next few days unless you're sound asleep in a hotel bed or some haystack. By yourself. Got it?"

As he drifted back from the dreamlike conversation with Silvano days earlier, he heard a voice, "Darik. Darik. You with me?" Lynetta said in a worried tone. "Whoever this Silvano is, he will just be happy you're not buried along the trail or eaten by critters who feast on burnt meat. Don't worry about the horse and wagon. They're replaceable. You're not! Naw, you survived something you shouldn't have. Not at all. And if you don't mind, I'm thinking that I'd like to see one of these birdhouses when you're healed up."

He smiled. "Wish I could, but the tools my grandfather gave me were in the buckboard. I suspect they were destroyed."

She nodded to Ingrid, "Sweetheart, go get it. Bring it here."

The beautiful young woman walked away and to Darik's surprise returned moments later carrying the satchel containing his tools.

"Darik, I was astonished these tools weren't destroyed. Makes no sense. Not really. There's clearly something mystical about them, some qualities we humans don't understand. At least I don't. So, how about we make a deal? You ain't going nowhere for a few weeks, maybe longer. Your burns are bad but you've already begun healing up a bit since last night. How about I find you a chunk of wood on the plateau, wood that speaks to me, and you carve me a birdhouse? I'll trade you the nursing and food as well as getting you some new clothes, and you do your carving. And by the way, your boots are fine. Maybe even protected you. Don't know why they didn't get a scratch on 'em."

Darik smiled as he and Ingrid looked eye to eye, something that did not go unnoticed by Lynetta. However, the young man's expression displayed extreme discomfort and exhaustion, and without another word he closed his eyes and drifted back into the world of dreams where he had spent much of the prior few days.

Storm clouds featuring a massive thunderhead emitted a mesmerizing floral fragrance that caused him to stop running so he could inhale the exotic smell. He heard voices that were not attached to any human forms but rather to falling leaves and wobbling tree limbs as a steady north wind moved with the tempo of a waltz. He was back in the same general store he had dreamed about numerous times over the prior two years, but this time he was standing face to face with a blonde-haired angel absent of her wings and naked as a baby at birth. Her arms were extended outward as though she wanted him to grab her hands, which he did. The female creature possessed marbled grayish-green eyes with traces of blue. He found himself unable or unwilling to fight off the seduction of his soul that she initiated. She pulled him forward gently, and his own body, suddenly naked, pressed against her warm, silken flesh as his aroused penis penetrated deep into the warm center of her most sexual place. He exploded inside her as their conjoined bodies floated horizontally at treetop level. She was lying atop his young torso and whispering loving phrases in a language he did not know.

CHAPTER 4
Recollection

At the sheriff's suggestion, Lynetta had sent a letter to the Eagle Trail Ranch with the mail carried on the stagecoach making daily runs to and from Castle Rock and points north all the way to Denver. She anticipated it would take several days for the letter to reach Eagle Trail to inform the ranch's owner that Darik was injured and had not run off with the horses and buckboard.

A return letter from Darik's boss arrived nine days later. "Your boss and this Silvano fellow must really have a liking for you. They was worried sick. Figured you hadn't run off. Thought some bandit might have killed you. Your boss, this Mulroony fella, says for you to stay put until you're healed up. Even sent me a twenty-dollar gold piece to pay for your room and board. Sonny, that's pretty special."

Darik was stunned. "He did that?"

"Yep. Also said that they'd already checked the whorehouse and nobody'd seen you, so I figure you're one hell of a reliable young man or those girls were lying for you. Your boss said to tell you that someone else was picking up the ponies in Kiowa. I'd told him it'd be a few weeks before you could travel and get back to his ranch. He's good with that. That being the case, how's my birdhouse coming along?" she asked.

He reached into the satchel. "My hands aren't working right just yet. Might take me another week to make the headway I want. Lying in bed trying to carve is damn difficult. Think I'll do my carving on the porch from now on. I need some fresh air and daylight."

Lynetta stared in silence as he pulled the roughed out birdhouse from the bag. "Never, never imagined someone could turn wood like that. Even a Ute pipe maker I know don't carve so sweetly."

He handed the object to her. She ran her fingers over the outer surface, still somewhat rough, and then used her index finger to touch the interior. "The inside's already done. How'd you do that?"

"Mostly done," he answered. "Best to get the hard work on the inside done before getting to the outside. Grandfather said that was the secret to life, getting the inside of things, the soul, fixed up and then to concentrate on the outside, the part other people see. These small carving tools are made from metal that never gets dull, so they cut through wood like a warm knife through butter, particularly soft wood like the aspen block you gave me. Watch how easily I scoop out small pieces."

Lynetta watched intently as he took the birdhouse and used one of the curved-handled tools shaped like a tiny measuring cup to scoop out ball-shaped spheres half the size of a pea, one after the other, with virtually no effort.

The young woman with the woven blonde hair entered the room. Her blue eyes sparkled as Lynetta pointed to the birdhouse. "Honey, look what our houseguest did with those burned fingers. He's quite a magician."

Ingrid examined the birdhouse carefully. She smiled, turned and walked back into an adjacent room.

"Is she your daughter?" he asked Lynetta.

"Mine? Me someone's mother? No," she chuckled. "Not hardly. Never had an interest in settlin' down with a husband and havin' kids. Ingrid's my cousin's daughter. She's from a country called Holland. That's where my kin and I came from, but I managed to settle here in Colorado, right here in Castle Rock. Don't that beat all? Parents got to America and stayed put back east in Ohio, and then I came to Colorado a few years before gold was found near Denver in fifty-nine. Pretty primitive place back then."

"Yes, Holland," he answered. "I know of Holland. A little. Far from Romania but not far like Colorado. Lots of fishermen and many farmers like my grandfather. Lots of small hills and fields of beautiful tulip flowers."

"Tulips. I remember seeing acres of tulips when I was a child," she sighed. "I was twelve when we left Holland. We got to America in 1851, and then I got here to Colorado in 1857 just before winter. I been right here in Castle Rock all this time. Twenty-five years. And the wild times have been abundant. Yes, indeed, more wild times than you'd ever imagine."

"Not born here?" he asked.

"Naw, most everyone my age you meet out here, almost none of 'em were born here. My folks decided to pack up and leave Holland, but I never knew why. After our ship got to New York, they decided to move on to Ohio a year later. They stayed put to farm, but I came to Colorado in a wagon train with my older brother and his wife. They only stayed two years and then headed up to Oregon; at least that's what they planned. Never heard from them again. I lived the next few years with a minister and his wife, helping out with their kids and things at their little church. He was the only preacher in the area.

That's what happens out here. People come, people go, and that includes family. Can't get too sentimental. People out here act like tumbleweed."

"What's her name? I heard you say it to her, but I've forgotten," he said while again looking wistfully at the beautiful young woman as she came back into the room with a glass of water she placed on Darik's nightstand before leaving as rapidly as she entered.

"Ingrid. She's a bit younger than you, and she ain't been with no man yet, at least by herself if you know what I mean, and I got responsibility for her, so don't get no ideas. You're a good boy; at least I think so. But she don't know a thing about men, and I'm not teaching her until she learns more English."

"I can help her a little," he replied, "with the English. I began learning English back home from the old woman I told you about but started learning proper English on the ship to America and more during the time it took me to get to Colorado. I learned plenty over the years, at least enough to get by. My boss and his wife, she died a few years back, and Silvano helped me learn more."

"You've done well, my little pilgrim. Sure, you can help her with English, but Ingrid's an innocent. As for you? I really don't think you're all that innocent. Your boss's letter mentioned a whorehouse. I'm not judging you, but it worries me a bit because you have a twinkle in your eye like a man who's already been with plenty of women. So don't get no ideas. English lessons only. That'd be good."

Ingrid, as though on cue, returned to the guest room. Darik pointed to his chest and said, "Darik. I'm Darik."

The young girl smiled and said, "I know."

After exchanging another set of glances with her, he closed his eyes and began replaying more of the conversation with Silvano leading up to his ill-fated trip to Kiowa.

"Silvano," Darik asked hesitantly although he already knew the answer. "Can I go Thursday, day after tomorrow? Want to finish up the new tack room. Just need one more day, maybe two, and I'll be done."

Eagle Trail Ranch, measuring four thousand acres, was situated on prime grazing land between the railhead station in Littleton and the largest set of knolls ten miles south of Denver along Bear Creek, where only hours earlier Darik first met a beautiful young woman named Lihua. But based on Silvano's timetable, he realized the trip to Kiowa would preempt meeting the young woman again as the two of them had agreed to at the end of their initial conversation. He knew there was no way to contact her about his sudden trip to Kiowa and was concerned she would think he was unreliable if he failed to show up. He assumed she would be angry, but he had no recourse, short of losing his job, if he did not follow Silvano's orders.

"Fuck you, you little prick," Silvano had shouted at him. "Don't bullshit me. You probably already got some pussy lined up for the next few days. I can smell your bullshit a mile away. Nobody else around here even comes close! Anyway, scheduling's my job. Following orders is yours. Head out tomorrow before sunrise. No more backtalk. You understand me? Follow the Platte a couple miles south, and then take the main trail to Louviers. Stay at the hotel overnight. Here's five dollars for the room and a meal or two each direction in case you don't pack up enough from the pantry to keep you properly fed. It's for both directions, for the entire ride. Don't get fucking drunk neither. Don't fuck no whores. Don't let me and the boss down. Next sunrise, take the widest of the trails, the one running southeast from Louviers, and follow it to Castle Rock. And then it's maybe three hours to Kiowa. You should reach Double Canyon Ranch, the Firmans' place, by two o'clock Thursday if you don't mess up. Bunk overnight in their barn unless they offer you a bed in the bunkhouse, but don't be a bother. Got it? Head back

Friday at sunrise. Stay in Louviers on the way back same as on the way there. Be here Saturday before supper. Don't you fucking disappoint me and the boss. And leave the whores alone," Silvano had snapped in the tone of an overly demanding yet protective father.

Darik replayed his encounter days earlier with Silvano before a series of yawns overtook him just as Ingrid returned to refill his water glass. Within five minutes of telling her goodnight, his eyes closed as he drifted back to Silvano while piecing together more memories from the day before the lightning storm, in particular, his disappointment that the rendezvous with the young woman from the sunflower field did not occur as planned. He now remembered that he had been unable to think of a way to send a message to Lihua once Silvano had given him his orders, yet something inside him, a basic lack of understanding about how to deal with a woman who was not a prostitute, made him wonder what the polite thing to do was.

He remembered how elated he was as he rode away from Lihua earlier that afternoon, recalling that he had given her one of his unfinished birdhouses, one that was nearly complete, figuring that the small gift conveyed a strong signal about his intentions to see her again, not unlike leaving her a handful of wildflowers. He hoped she would realize that something had changed his schedule and would forgive him for not showing up as planned. But no matter how he tried to piece things together, he was uncertain how much time had elapsed since he spoke with her that first afternoon.

His mind wavered helplessly in a vacuum of time as he lay in bed. He remembered consuming a lighter than usual supper the night before he left for Kiowa: a chunk of nearly stale soda bread, black beans, and a leg of boiled chicken. It was all he could consume throughout that final meal as he pictured every detail of this beautiful young woman. Unsure as to why he was so enamored with her, especially since they had only spoken for a few minutes, he sensed, or at least hoped, she felt the same way about him. That was something new for him, to actually care that a woman displayed interest in him without him having to hand over money for the pleasure of her time.

He remembered reaching under his bed after dinner that final night and pulling out the leather-covered trunk with the satchel containing his tools. As he thought back to that first day, his mind drifted from one memory to the next with no apparent connection. He retraced memories of the wise woman in his Romanian village, an especially mysterious creature for an uneducated young farm boy like him to comprehend.

He recalled how difficult it was to lift the trunk with the satchel containing forty carving tools, his only real possessions, when he was a young boy traveling on his own to America from Romania.

A restless stirring continued as he meandered in and out of sleep while scattered, sharp bursts of pain bombarded him as he lay in the guest room bed. He remembered that he had begun carving several new birdhouses the week leading up to the lightning storm, one he was especially fond of that was made from a pristine piece of birch he was certain would last a lifetime if cured properly after the carving was completed. He loved the patterns on that block of wood but assumed it had been destroyed during the lightning storm.

During his final night at the ranch, his thoughts had alternated between the delicate, precise movements he was making with the sharp carving tools and the detailed image in his mind of the young woman in the field of sunflowers. But despite not being able to escape the memory of her beautiful face, he kept cutting, scooping, and shaping the birdhouse's interior, carving the block of wood from the inside out as efficiently as possible, following the precise technique taught to him by his grandfather. That last night at the ranch now seemed like ancient history.

Now, however, recuperating at Lynetta's home and just before he was about to enter into another dreamscape, he thought back to the morning he had left the ranch, after only five hours of sleep, and begun the first leg of his trip, what he thought would be an uneventful buckboard ride. Just as Silvano had directed, he had dropped off the old mare at the Louviers' livery on Thursday afternoon and enjoyed a decent meal and night's sleep at the only hotel in the small town without even considering stopping by the whorehouse.

As he again drifted on the edge of sleep, he remembered how he had felt confused, or at the very least, concerned the next morning as he hitched the horse to the buckboard and headed out to Kiowa.

29

He had visited this waterfall in another dream, but this time it was higher and more powerful. The fierce bubbling water fell endlessly into a riverbed so far below him that he could not see it through the cloudy mist. He heard a woman's voice, possibly that of his grandmother or possibly Lihua, crying out, begging for him to catch her. But he was blinded by the mist and reached out helplessly, his arms extended, his hands opened, but could not feel anyone. His fingertips began to burn as the pressure of the water pounded his hands. He could see blisters had formed on his hands, grotesque, nasty looking sections of discolored flesh. As the water fell hundreds of feet downward, it was transformed into thin streaks of fire moving at high speed like crisscrossing lightning bolts bouncing off the banks of the river and the walls of the crevice now containing the watery fire. He jumped into the cloud but did not fall downward. Instead, he floated like a feather above the water, tossing and turning out of control.

CHAPTER 5
Kindred

He drifted in and out of dreams until awakening the next morning, continuing to reflect upon that chance meeting with the beautiful girl in a field north of Littleton. *How long ago was that?* he wondered. He had lost track of time since he arrived at Lynetta's.

"Lihua. Her name was Lihua," he heard himself whisper in a way that would preclude him from forgetting it ever again.

He willed the image of her into sharper focus and remembered that the sun had been about twenty degrees above the western horizon the first time he saw her in the field. As the afternoon sun traveled slowly to the west, its curtain of light crawled over a foreground of wildflowers and tall grasses, further defined by a backdrop of emerald green foothills and low-slung mountaintops stretching as far to the north and south as his eyes could see.

As his burns continued to heal, he lay in Lynetta's guest room bed on what he estimated was the ninth or tenth day since the lightning storm. He realized he had no idea which day of the month it really was nor which month. Embarrassed by the memory loss, he chose not to ask either Lynetta or Ingrid about the actual date, hoping he would figure it out.

The days passed with increased speed as he replayed the details of the sunlight passing through the young woman's ankle-length dress the afternoon they met and how it carved out a magical silhouette of her body through the fabric in a way that revealed her torso as though she were naked. He initially felt he had been trespassing by staring secretively at her as the sun's backlighting illuminated her body.

He remembered how the gold pocket watch that once belonged to his grandfather had chimed a soft, almost inaudible note that first afternoon, signifying the bottom of the hour, and how he realized an hour had passed since he first witnessed this young goddess performing her slow waltz in the field with him as the only audience.

Tired from journeying back and forth in his dreams, his memories became more blurred, yet he entered into a more lucid dreamlike state as his body continued to come to terms with pain that diminished with each sunrise and sunset.

That was then and this is now, he reconciled in his thoughts as he slowly recovered from the serious injuries. Nonetheless, having had his breath taken away by a total stranger was not something he would ever release from his heart. He was curious and somewhat doubtful whether he would ever again see the young woman in the field, feeling as though such a perfect moment might never present itself.

He recalled how amazed he had been that first afternoon when he turned directly toward the mysterious woman and waved involuntarily, and how she, at the same moment, turned, looked into his eyes, and waved back. He had been stunned, feeling himself transformed instantly into a granite-like statue with a moving arm as they gestured to one another.

Why would she wave at me, a total stranger? What am I supposed to do? he had thought at the time, as his ox-hide cowboy boots felt like they were bolted to the ground.

They then closed the gap of thirty yards in gentle strides, seeming to float an inch about the ground. Her hazel eyes were welded to his blue eyes. Their mouths, first tightly bound, had relaxed into beautifully expansive smiles that for him generated sensations he was not prepared to experience.

"Darik. Darik Jacoby," he had said as they drew within a few feet of one another.

"Lihua," she replied without sharing her family name.

He reached into his vest pocket and double-checked the timepiece. It was time for him to walk back to his horse and return to the ranch so he would be able to have supper and get a reasonable night's sleep before beginning Silvano's assignment the next morning. The internal conflict he had experienced by not wanting this unexplainable interlude with Lihua to conclude was strong, but he finally asked her, "Tomorrow? Here? Same time?"

"Cannot. Two days? Yes?" she had replied.

They extended their right arms, seemingly in slow motion, and their hands came together in a tight grip that generated sensations that caused time to stand still as powerful feelings of passion moved through his body.

"Yes," they answered one another in unison. "Two days."

Then a thought suddenly occurred to him. "Wait here. Wait a minute. Don't move. Please. Just wait. I'll be right back. Please wait for me."

"Why wait?" she asked. But before answering, he sprinted back to his horse, hopped up onto the saddle and rode back to where Lihua stood. He dismounted and reached into the saddlebag as he pulled out a small carved wooden object which she did not recognize.

He noticed her confused look. "It's a birdhouse. Do you know what a birdhouse is?" he had asked.

"Birdhouse? For little birds in trees. Birdhouse."

"Yes. I carved it. It's what I do in my spare time. I want you to have it. Will you accept it as a….gift?" he asked hesitantly.

"Accept? Gift?"

"Not trying to be pushy, Miss, but it somehow feels like it's supposed to belong to you. It's not finished. Still needs some work. Please keep it until we meet up again, and then you can let me know what you want me to do to make it perfect. Listen to it for a moment. It's got a song you need to hear," he added.

He recalled placing his lips within an inch of the oval-shaped opening on the front of the birdhouse, and as he blew across it, she appeared stunned by the sound of a bird chirping a soft, delicate song, seeming to come out from within the birdhouse.

She had not understood all his words but seemed delighted with the birdsong. "Yes. Xièxiè. Accept it," she responded.

"Yours. Yes. When we meet up again, I'll take a little time to finish it up for you just the way you want. Doesn't need much work, just a little," he told her.

"Thank you. It beautiful."

He remembered staring at her with a long and silent smile before remounting his horse. "Yes. Beautiful. Like you." He then pulled the reins to his left and rode away slowly, turning back and waving one more time.

CHAPTER 6
Sendoff

On the twenty-seventh day after the lightning strike, Darik prepared to board the stagecoach that would take him to the Littleton railhead after brief stops in Louviers and then at a weigh station south of Littleton where multiple stage routes intersected, not far from the convergence of several large irrigation canals that fed the South Platte River. Lynetta purchased his ticket from the money Darik's boss had sent after learning of his injury.

Darik hugged Lynetta, kissed her on both cheeks, and then did the same with Ingrid, whose skills in English had increased dramatically during the past month. Just as he was about to enter the passenger compartment, he reached out and presented the completed birdhouse to Lynetta.

"Wonder of wonders," she chuckled. "Thought you might try sneaking out of town without me getting this birdhouse. It's the most beautiful carving on God's green earth. I'll cherish it forever. You're now kin to me, Darik. You can be a son, nephew, cousin, or just a friend, whatever suits you. You come back soon or I'll come to the ranch and drag you back!"

Ingrid stared into Darik's eyes. They had begun to share sensations of childlike joy, feelings that increased in depth and intensity each afternoon during her informal English lessons or when they strolled Lynetta's property. Neither had ever experienced a real friendship with someone of the opposite sex, yet their mannerisms and personalities fit together like a hand in a glove. She possessed a gentle loving kindness he embraced, and though he tried to deny it to himself and avoided the subject when Lynetta had casually asked him about it one time, he knew he had fallen in love with the young Dutch woman in a very different manner compared to what every cell in his body told him about the feelings of love, smitten at first sight, he had for the young Chinese woman weeks earlier. But Darik forced his thoughts about Lihua into the background during his stay at Lynetta's, at least when he was near Ingrid. At other times his thoughts returned to the sunflower field where he had met Lihua. It was the first time in his life he had experienced any form of an emotional conflict about a woman, in this case two women he cared for deeply, something not permitted with the prostitutes in Louviers.

Through the open window of the stagecoach, Darik reached out to Ingrid's extended arm and handed her a smaller birdhouse, one carved from linden. The limb from which he cut the block was moist and his small carving tools had scooped and shaped the wood effortlessly. He told Ingrid to place the small birdhouse on a window ledge with indirect sunlight for several weeks where it could cure properly.

"I'll be back, I promise," he shouted as the six horses pulling the stagecoach began to reach full stride and stirred up a small cloud of dust.

Darik daydreamed as the vehicle handled the meandering curves on the relatively flat roadway with ease. The suspension on the stagecoach was better than on the boss's buckboard, now destroyed, but speed amplified every bump and pothole. Like the other passengers, he bounced up and down throughout the journey, and because he was not fully healed from his month-old injuries, each bounce fueled remnants of pain that he did his best to ignore.

To offset the rigors of the ride and discomfort he was experiencing, he daydreamed about Lihua and wondered what it was that moved him so deeply about her? He had no answer, not one that made sense. Was he entirely enamored of her beauty, or was it her gentleness or were there mystical qualities that had entrapped him that he could not comprehend, especially since they had only spoken briefly? He sensed she felt the same way towards him although their instant infatuation was not logical by anything he could gauge against it. He recalled how worried he had been a month earlier that the Kiowa trip ordered by Silvano would preempt meeting with Lihua the next day and hoped for another opportunity to be with her.

Now, nearly thirty days later and aboard a stagecoach taking him home, his concerns about ever seeing her again had not lessened.

CHAPTER 7
Reappearance

Two horsemen familiar to Darik, Michael Mulroony, his boss and the ranch's owner, and Andreas Silvano, the ranch's foreman, were waiting at the stage depot with the reins of another horse in hand.

"Don't just stand there, Sonny," Silvano chirped. "Let's get going."

"Boss! Silvano!" he said excitedly. "I was going to walk to the ranch. Not expecting this at all."

Mulroony, a tall and cultivated silver-haired Irishman who came to America from Cork, Ireland, as a twenty-nine year old in 1863, just smiled. After settling briefly in Harrisburg, Pennsylvania, he had enlisted in the Union Army and then four years later moved on to Colorado. Mulroony looked at Darik and replied, "Laddie, not sure why you've been graced with such glorious strength, but anyone who survives a lightning strike is worth having at my ranch. As long as you continue to work like you've done since you first arrived here and don't take Silvano's insults too personally, you've got a home on my ranch as long as you like. And by the way, Silvano, once a man of the cloth or so he claims when he's drunk, doesn't like Irishmen any more than Romanians, especially Jewish ones. Then again, he doesn't like them any less. Only reason he likes me is because I pay his wages on time."

Darik mounted the horse, nodded, reached out to shake Mulroony's hand and then felt Silvano's powerful grip on his shoulder as the burly man wearing a colorful Mexican poncho reached out with his other hand and gave Darik a pat on the cheek in a fatherly manner.

"I'll pay you back for the buckboard and pony. I let you down," Darik commented in an apologetic tone, but the older men laughed, simply relieved that the younger man was alive.

The threesome followed the main trail for several miles, eventually reaching Eagle Trail's main gate. They dismounted and Darik led the horses to the main corral where the stableboy took charge of two of the animals and placed their saddles, blankets, and bridles in the tack room.

Darik led his horse back to Mulroony and Silvano who were in the midst of an animated conversation.

"Boss, sorry to interrupt," he said, "but I have to take care of something important. I'm a month late doing it. I'll be back by nightfall, I promise."

"Don't let no lightning stop you this time," Silvano replied as the boss tapped the brim of his hat in approval.

Darik had kept the satchel with his wood carving tools on his lap throughout the stagecoach ride and now tied the leather pouch to the saddle horn and began his ride toward the field of sunflowers, carrying with him an image of a young Chinese woman he held close to his heart.

Thinking back to his childhood experiences in the Romanian forests and his interactions with trees and the guidance they provided him, he admitted that he had stopped listening and had allowed himself to become preoccupied with his life on the ranch and not much else. He also thought back to the old crone, Baba, and how often she had advised him to avoid making presumptions as he grew older if he were going to deal successfully with love, fear, or the pain and suffering that he, like most people, would likely experience at one time or another.

CHAPTER 8
Harken

Although he had no way to know if Lihua would be there this time, during his ride back to the sunflower field he revisited thoughts of their first meeting. They flooded his mind, every detail as fresh as the moment when he and the beautiful young woman first met.

"Attend. Attune. Be aware," he heard a wispy, familiar voice interrupt his thoughts, a voice that seemed to come from a stand of piñon pines. "Listen. Attune," the voice advised. "Be reminded. Never forget."

"You got it all wrong this time," he shouted at the top of his lungs toward the trees, hearing his voice echo, certain that the tree was incorrect. "I didn't listen last time and that was my mistake. I wasn't paying attention, but you've got this wrong. Blue sky today. No lightning. Any fool can see that. I'm hopefully going to get to see her again. Don't bother me!"

His thoughts drifted back a month when he witnessed orange-colored sunbeams piercing the afternoon sky, tantalizing him as the rays backlit the silhouetted torso of the mysterious young woman with almond-shaped eyes standing less than a hundred feet away, a vision of beauty who seemed to be awash in her own daydreams.

He wondered if she had even noticed he had been watching her.

I must have looked like an idiot that day, he thought to himself. *Other than the little girls in my village and my grandmother, and then on the wagon train, I've never really tried to meet a woman who wasn't a whore. She had to have noticed I was nervous, probably as nervous as she was. But something inside told me she was the woman I was supposed to be with, and that's the oddest thing that's ever happened. How would I know what it is to fall in love? I have no clue,* he concluded.

CHAPTER 9
Enchantment

Darik kept up a moderate canter during the ride, arriving at the sunflower field just after two o'clock. The sun was high above the crest of the foothills to the west. Though he realized there was little chance she would be there, he was not deterred.

He dismounted and led his horse over the knoll where he and Lihua first spoke with one another and where he later handed her the small birdhouse.

He noticed movement among the tall golden-yellow sunflower blossoms, many of which topped six feet. Their tall stalks turned to the west as they followed the path of the afternoon sun. He assumed it was a coyote or a stray dog moving through the sunflowers, but when a human figure arose, he recognized that the silhouette belonged to a familiar looking woman with long black hair that reached to her waist.

He stared in silence briefly before saying, "I'm back."

She turned. She held the small birdhouse in her hand. "I knew you coming today. Birdhouse told me. I listened. I knew it. I knew you hurt. I knew you not dead. I knew."

He smiled as he attempted to display calm although his heart pounded rapidly. "Do you know what lightning is?"

She nodded. "Yes."

"I was hit. The buckboard and horse were destroyed. I was burned pretty bad. Been resting up in a little town called Castle Rock this whole time. Maybe twenty-five miles from here. I saw you in my dreams. I saw you several times. It seemed like all the time. Please say your name again. I want to hear you say it."

"Lihua," she answered lovingly as he could see his reflection in her eyes, something that calmed him instantly. "Time to finish birdhouse. Know what want. Please carve both names on roof to see forever. Want forever."

"Yes. Forever. I'll carve them. Do you know how to spell your name?"

"Yes. It spelled L-i-h-u-a. Lihua."

"Mine is spelled D-a-r-i-k. Darik."

"Where from?"

"Romania. Far away. Across the Atlantic Ocean. What does your name mean? Where are you from?"

"China. Across other ocean. Grandmother name me. Means *powerful beauty*," she said as she lowered her eyes modestly.

"Looks like we've both found ourselves here in Colorado. Two foreigners who traveled all the way across different oceans just so we could meet here again today. How about that! A Romanian man and a Chinese woman who were total strangers a month ago, but now our names will be carved onto the top of your birdhouse forever. What are you going to do with it?" he asked.

"Found special place in forest. Put there. Healthy trees. Not tall, not yet. Grow fast. I show."

She led him by the left hand as his right hand pulled the reins. Her touch produced a pulsating sensation that raced through his body as they entered a thicket along the north bank of Bear Creek. There, to his surprise, was a small pond less than fifty feet in diameter adjacent to a group of trees that included linden, massive ponderosa pines, and dozens of leafy cottonwoods and maples. His heart pounded from the sight like it did when he and his grandfather explored the forested areas outside Bucharest.

"There," she said while pointing to an isolated stand of silver maple trees covered in a mosaic of green, red, brown, and gold autumn leaves. "One of those."

"Silver maple," he commented. "They grow well in this river basin. Wood's softer than oak or elm, and it's prettier than the cottonwoods lining the banks of Bear Creek and the small streams around here. It's a good choice, but I think a cottonwood would be better for the long haul. Cottonwoods do better in the winter than these soft maples. Do you mind if I pick one? Is it all right if we put it on a cottonwood?"

"Yes. Fine. You pick. Please pick. Not know trees."

"I have an idea," he replied. "Let's get you onto the saddle and we'll ride around until we find a small cottonwood that speaks to you. Is that okay?"

Having no idea what he meant by a tree speaking to her, she nodded out of courtesy.

He placed his hands around her waist and told her to jump as he lifted her atop the saddle, carefully placing her in a side-saddle position. He experienced a sudden feeling of intimacy when he placed his hands on her waist and sensed she was shy by nature. He hoped she was not uncomfortable. *This ain't like dancing with a woman at a square dance,* he thought to himself. *Something's different and she seems to trust me right now much more than I trust myself. I want her, but this feels different. I need to treat her perfectly, treat her like an angel. I don't get what's happening to me.*

"How's that?" he finally asked. "I won't let the horse go faster than a walk."

"You walk?" she asked. "You ride. Your horse. I get down."

Darik had already considered this possibility before lifting her up, but was not sure how to accommodate her request because their bodies would be pressed together if they shared the saddle.

"Naw. Stay put. We'll fit on the saddle if that's what you want. You sure about this?" he asked in a gentlemanly tone.

"Yes," she replied cautiously.

"Then turn a little and slide toward the horse's neck so there'll be enough room for me."

She scooted forward a few inches. Her right hip rested against the saddle horn. Darik placed his left boot in the stirrup, lifted himself with his left hand gripping the horn, and without touching her, he flung his right leg over the back of the saddle.

He landed softly but slid forward an inch more than he had planned. His thighs were pressed lightly against her left hip, and the body heat generated by their contact was intense, hypnotically so, as they both remained silent. He placed his right boot in the far stirrup, which caused his chest to press against her shoulder, but rather than move forward, she leaned back and pressed her shoulders against his chest. Despite wanting to be the perfect gentleman, he was aroused. However, this was more akin to the lightness of being he had experienced in his many daydreams, certainly different from how he felt during his numerous visits to the brothel in Louviers.

They stared at one another for an instant as their juxtaposition on the saddle took their breath away. He reached both arms around her as he held the reins, and the horse moved slowly toward the large section of cottonwoods.

Not a word was uttered. With his body pressing against hers, he was certain she was now leaning back against him with greater pressure. He watched her torso rocking gently back and forth in a slow, syncopated motion identical to the horse's movements as they sauntered towards the trees.

His face moved within an inch of her left cheekbone, and he inhaled her fragrance, wondering what she was thinking. Was she experiencing the same intense warmth moving through her body as he was? Did she have the same curious desire to surrender to him as much as he wanted her? He sensed this was a territory into which she had likely never ventured, largely based on what he assumed to be her age, yet he felt a level of self-doubt of his own in addition to strong pangs of lust.

"Welcome, Darik," he heard a voice whisper from one of the cottonwoods. "Yes, this is the one."

Fearful of alarming her if he responded aloud to the tree's encouraging words, he nodded approvingly but remained silent.

"There," he pointed. "Those two saplings. Young trees with thick trunks for their height. Either one'll work. Barely over six feet. Strong enough to withstand the baby bears, and hopefully the bigger ones, too, at least in a year or two. You just never know. If we mount the birdhouse near the top of one of them, by next spring that cottonwood will be at least four to six feet taller and the birdhouse won't be able to be reached by most four-legged critters other than squirrels, especially with it in the middle of the stand. In a couple years, it'll be a fifteen or twenty footer and the birdhouse will be safe forever."

"Good. I like. Do another day? Carve names and put birdhouse there another day?"

He smiled. "My tools are right here." He pointed to the satchel. "I can carve our names right now. They'll look perfect. I can do it with you on the saddle, then I'll attach the birdhouse to the tree so it'll never come down."

"Yes, long time," she said as they pressed against one another a little more forcefully and his lips brushed her left ear. He felt her shudder.

The leaves in the trees began to rustle, and Darik could hear them singing a soft, almost imperceptible song of love and truth, "You have found your mate, your true love, but you do not yet realize it," he heard the female voice of a tree say in a giggle. "She is as pure as an angel. Your hearts are one. Do no harm. Stay true."

"You're right. I think you're right. She is the one," he responded silently to the tree. "She is the one."

Darik noticed that Lihua's shyness had begun to shift, at least a little, to the confidence of a grown woman. She looked at him and said, "Day we meet, I not know what to think. When young girl, Grandmother said I meet handsome man someday and heart pound like drum."

"Is that what happened that day?" he asked. "Your heart felt like a drum beating? Did you know I'd been staring at you the whole time we were in the field?"

She smiled. "Thought so. Thought you stare. You stand behind me. Warm sunshine in our faces. You not look like boy. You older. Hoped eyes blue. Not know why. Hoped."

"Blue. They're blue. You were right. Good guess."

"Saw hand cover eyes from sunlight," she explained as her hand moved into the position of a salute.

"The sun was so bright that day," he replied, "and I noticed you were doing the same thing…raising your hand up to your eyes to block the sun. I have to admit that this, right now, what we're doing, is the first time I've ever spoken with a Chinese person about anything that mattered. Definitely the first time I've ever spoken with a beautiful Chinese woman. And never in my life with anyone as beautiful as you. Never."

She blushed. "For me not proper to stare at stranger. Wonder what you think? Wonder if because I Chinese or you think I pretty? Did not know. Was afraid. A little."

"Are you still afraid? I hope not."

Darik carefully worded his next set of questions to avoid confusing her. As a result, she told him in broken English about the thoughts and feelings she had that first afternoon and how, when she saw him standing in the same intense sunlight, it made her so nervous that she could not move even a fraction of an inch.

She told him that on the day they first met she had just washed her hair, and, as she often did, dried it by running through the field where she and Darik now stood. She told him that she loved the way the breeze caressed the long black hair that covered her entire back when untied.

He guided the horse to the second tree, the one earmarked for the birdhouse. "This one looks perfect. Thick young trunk. Limbs are strong and healthy. I'm pretty sure that this one will outlive us, our children, and their children."

"Children?" she said with a look of surprise.

Caught off guard by her response, he tried to backtrack. "I didn't mean it that way. I meant that the tree and the birdhouse will outlive us and any children either of us might have if and when either of us ever settles down and has a family. Does that make sense?"

By the blank look on her face, it was clear she did not comprehend his rambling explanation, but he remembered what she had already shared about her grandmother's words and found himself hoping that he might actually be the man of her dreams. While he had no real way of knowing what she was feeling or thinking, he began to think she was, in fact, his dream come true.

"Never alone with man," she volunteered. "Never kiss before now." Without another word she leaned towards him in a very deliberate manner and placed a gentle kiss upon his lips.

He was so stunned that his lips did not soften when hers touched his. He kept his hands motionless as his thoughts vaulted him into a place that seemed as though he was watching these events through a looking glass at the same moment he was feeling the actual sensations of her warm lips pressed against his. He felt as though he was in a dream, one of his inexplicable nightly dreams that often left him confused. But he knew this was occurring now and not part of a lavish dreamscape.

He smiled and whispered, "I've never had a kiss quite like that before. See," he tried to explain, "the others I've had were a lot different, especially the ones I got from my grandmother when she'd tuck me into bed at night."

She laughed and he knew right then that she did not believe him.

"Only with grandmother? Only? Not that kind of kiss, Darik. Not that kind."

Without another word, their lips came together softly in a way that would engrave their souls for a lifetime. Their eyes were riveted together. He held her tightly and as they moved their lips apart ever so briefly, he memorized the look in her eyes.

Darik then removed a small wooden carving tool from the satchel hanging by his right calf, a fine tipped, V-shaped blade attached to a black wooden handle worn into the shape of his grip. With his other arm wrapped around her and with the birdhouse now resting in her lap, he began the delicate process of carving their names. While his left hand held the birdhouse steady, his wrist and forearm pressing against the upper most part of her left leg, he carved her name slowly, letter by letter. The heat radiating from her leg was intense as the mating dance he and Lihua were performing was natural and uninhibited. The sensations were more powerful than anything he had ever experienced.

He was certain she was a virgin and sensed she had no practical knowledge of what to do next, yet to his surprise, she instinctively moved her legs apart a fraction of an inch so that the lower portion of his left wrist rested just above the convergence of her thighs. She patted his forearm softly and remained silent. All he could think about was not hurting this young woman, not violating her life, yet he felt conflicted about what he should do next.

Even with the distraction of his arm pressing against her in such an intimate way, the carving of each letter, L-i-h-u-a and then D-a-r-i-k, took less than fifteen minutes. He went deep enough into the wood surface, at least a half inch, so that no amount of wind, rain, snow or sunshine would erode the lettering during this lifetime or the next.

"What do you think? Do you like how our names look?"

"Yes. So graceful," she replied. "Reminds me of Chinese letters."

He asked her more questions about their chance meeting that first afternoon including why her hair was now woven into a tight, long braid that reached to the top of her tiny waist. She told him that it was practical because the braid would not interfere with her housekeeping duties at the Brown's summer home, a Victorian mansion located a quarter mile away that neither could see from this section of the sunflower field.

"What did you think when we began talking that day?" he asked, still wondering about the depth of his feelings for this woman and his lingering self-doubt about being around someone so innocent, albeit someone for whom he felt such strong pangs of lust. *What should I do? Should I stop and hold back? What am I supposed to do?*

She interrupted his internal debate. "You not look like other cowboys. Different. Far away eyes. Not know why. Are you homesick?"

"Some people call what you have *intuition*," he replied. "Do you know the word?"

"No."

"Well, it's knowing things without anyone telling you anything about them. It's when you sense something before it happens. I've known a couple of other women in my life like that, like you. There was an old woman in my village who was kind of magical, and then there's Lynetta, the woman who saved me after the lightning. They see the future. I think you can too. Think about it, Lihua. You said that the birdhouse told you I was coming back today. Did you mean the birdhouse actually told you like we are talking now, or do you just have a special way of knowing things without words? Maybe both. And, sure, I've always thought trees and my birdhouses were kind of magical in how they speak to me, but you just might have the kind of magic like those other women, and you can sometimes see bits and pieces of the future."

She raised her eyebrows slightly and hunched her shoulders, her way of expressing, "I don't know what to say."

In forced, somewhat stilted English, she tried to tell him about her life in China as well as the challenges she faced once her ship docked in San Francisco three years earlier. She told him that she and her older sister came to America together with nothing more than a few basic necessities that fit snugly into matching, hand-embroidered travel bags made by their grandmother. Each girl's bag also contained a silk robe and wedding gown also crafted by their grandmother, someone they knew they would never hug again once they boarded the ship to America.

She struggled to explain what she was thinking when she first saw Darik the day they met, how she had looked around to see if there was something else in the field that had captured his attention, adding that she doubted he had noticed her. She repeated that the bright sun that afternoon caused her to squint and that was why she had raised her hand to her forehead.

"You thought I was looking at something else? That's funny," he responded. "I could only see you. Nothing else."

Her smile widened. "Wonder if you see me different from other women? Wonder if I only look like simple Chinese girl? I hope you see more. Hope you now see me as grown woman with good heart."

In what he thought was surprisingly bold and seemingly out of character, she again mentioned that she had never been with a man, not by herself, not in China or San Francisco, nor in her new home in Colorado while working for the wealthy Mrs. Brown whose country estate was a half-dozen miles southwest of Denver, only an hour horseback ride from the base of foothills bordering the Rocky Mountains. It seemed to Darik that Lihua's life had changed dramatically over the past thirty-six months, and he was as curious about this woman as he was excited.

"Do all American men stare at women they not know?"

"If a man's really polite and not too obvious," he answered in a joking tone, albeit with his brows furrowing in tandem and a serious facial expression, "then it's kind of normal as long as the woman's boyfriend or her husband or father or overly protective brothers aren't nearby." Her puzzled expression indicated she did not understand his sense of humor.

She told him that she had wondered how his voice might sound if they actually spoke that first afternoon and that she also wondered if he was simply a handsome young cowboy—the most handsome man she had ever seen—or something else, someone of extraordinary talent and skills.

"I shy. Hope I understand what you say. Took long time to understand Mrs. Brown so I can do job right way. You have problems to talk American?"

He shook his head slowly, "Naw."

Without her grandmother there to ask, Lihua admitted that she did not know the words to describe the sensations that rushed through her that first afternoon, and she also admitted that this second conversation was not much easier.

He placed his hand on her shoulder to help her relax. "I can't explain what's happening," Darik commented. "What this is. Not at all. This is also very different for me."

"Why?" she asked.

"I'm just a cowboy. I'm mostly a carpenter at the ranch. Things are raw and pretty basic out here for the men at the ranch. We do our jobs and don't earn much money, but the freedom is powerful. See, a man like me just follows his instincts, his gut, and no matter what else you might think about me, I've never really spoken with a woman like we're doing. Not honest like this. It feels good. Really good. And I don't want you to be fearful of me or this at all. Okay?"

"Yes. I not know what you think when I wave. Wonder. Hope."

"Me too. I wondered what was happening. Didn't know what I was supposed to do next. I was scared to death."

She blushed and tipped her head slightly to one side.

He told her that when they both stopped waving at the same time that day in the sunflower field, it brought back the memory of two dancers performing in a beautiful ballet at the summer festival in Bucharest years earlier, adding that when they began walking toward one another that day, his body vibrated from head to toe.

It felt like I was floating an inch above the field's surface when I began walking toward you, he said to himself while doing his utmost to memorize her every word and gesture, curious about her response to him sharing his innermost thoughts and feelings. *And the closer I got to you and saw how your eyes were locked onto mine, I remember that I began to smile with my whole body. I remember how that smile felt,* he recalled in his thoughts.

Darik now found himself detached from the reality of the moment as he continued describing their first encounter. "Darik. Darik Jacoby," I blurted, "and then I felt like I was in some sort of powerful dream when you immediately replied, "Lihua.""

Once again demonstrating a level of assertiveness he did not expect from such a shy person, she told him that she had liked the way he looked atop his golden horse and how she was taken by his confident expression and that when he dismounted and reached into the saddlebag she was stunned to see him pull out the birdhouse.

"You had no idea what it was," he said, "at least that's what it looked like to me. And then I told you it was a birdhouse and asked if you knew what I meant."

She told him that she had not understood all his words that first afternoon nor how a birdhouse could make such sounds, but he remembered that she immediately responded, "Yes. Accept it. Thank you."

By the pleasant, somewhat calm expression she displayed that afternoon, Darik also had assumed it might have been the first gift she had ever received from a man.

She then told him that when he rode away a month earlier and she held the carved object, her heart had exploded with joy as she returned to Mrs. Brown's house, all the while hoping that the ten-minute walk would allow her enough time to regain her composure.

"When I rode away that afternoon," he reminisced, "it occurred to me that you might have thought I was just some worthless cowhand, you know, some sort of drifter who was just trying to, well, make advances on you. That worried me a lot."

"What mean?" she asked.

"Some men I know, well, even me when I was younger, when we see a beautiful woman, we get this urge to just grab the gal, give her a kiss, and see what happens next."

"Not understand what happens next?" she replied innocently.

Undeterred by her response, Darik tried to think of a way to answer that would both make sense and not offend her. "Well, when a man and a woman have these kind of feelings, just like other creatures do when they see one they really like a lot, sometimes they mate with each other or they think they should. Sometimes they mate to make babies. Sometimes they mate just because it feels real good. It just depends on the animals or the people. Does that make sense? You understand mating?"

She smiled. "Yes. Mating. Understand. Same in China. But girls I know in China marry before mating. Most. Not all. Most. American people mate first?"

"Hmm. Some yes, some no," he said with a tinge of doubt in his voice. "Some men, well, in fact, most the ones I know, they do it, the mating, because it brings pleasure. And even some women I know, they do it for money, you know, prostitutes, but I'm not judging them. It's their choice to do whatever they want. Some folks might not want children, not ever, but they like the mating. I can't blame them, especially if they don't want a family. Not sure how anyone else looks at this, at mating, but I'm sure there's really not a wrong or right purpose. I suppose there are religious people who'd disagree with me, but I just don't think it matters either way, not if two people trust each other and want to be together that way. And I'm sorry if this might make me seem crude."

"Crude?"

"Well, I don't want you to think that my feelings about you are dishonest. But down deep I think two adults should make their own decisions about things like this without others interfering or passing judgment."

He could see that this part of their meandering discussion made little sense to her and was relieved when she again changed the subject. Darik thought this might be due to her feeling embarrassed about the topic of mating. In fact, he was reasonably sure of it.

She continued to describe how, after she had finished walking from the field where they met that first afternoon, she returned to her bedroom in the servant quarters and placed the birdhouse on top of her dresser.

With a faraway look in her eye, she told him that after dinner that night, long after the sun had set and she tried to fall asleep, she felt something radiating from the birdhouse, something she could not describe. Nothing else she had ever been near had the magnetic power of that carved object. She told him that she stared at it for a few moments, rose from bed, walked to the dresser, lifted the small birdhouse into her hand and returned to bed clutching it tightly. She rubbed her fingers over its smooth surface and slid her index finger into the hollowed out object, amazed at its perfect smoothness. She held the birdhouse close to the lantern on the nightstand and, for the first time, saw that the interior was as beautiful as the exterior.

"I'm pleased that you like it so much," he said. "Wasn't at all sure what you thought about it. Not like I gave you a bouquet of flowers."

"Like much." she replied. "Better than flowers. Put birdhouse on pillow and watch until sleepy. In dreams saw you on horse sitting behind me. Held me tight. Like now."

"I believe in dreams. I trust them," Darik said with a knowing glance. "I love the stories in my dreams. New stories each night. They're important to me, and it was the same for my grandfather. How about you? A dreamer?"

"Yes. Dream a lot. Not understand. But like."

He finished the lettering and she nodded with approval. She then turned slowly, placed her lips upon his once again, and he released the birdhouse from his grip as his left hand lingered atop the small gap between her legs as the birdhouse rested on her thighs. Through the cotton fabric, it felt to him as though nothing separated his hand from her skin. Her tongue traced the surface of his lips, and he reciprocated although it tickled them both a little. From her expression, Darik thought he could see a powerful surge of energy moving through her, and it appeared she liked the sensation.

His right hand held the carving tool as tightly as possible while she pressed his left hand softly just above the vortex of her legs.

After bracing the carving tool against the saddle horn without looking away from her, his right hand slid gently up and down her blouse, seductively gliding it over and down her shoulders and then lightly across the outside of each breast. He then lowered his hands below her waistline, placing them atop her own hands, and they then moved together just below her belly.

Darik was not sure if he was seducing an innocent young woman under false pretenses or if what he was feeling was the kind of passion he had heard about but doubted actually existed, the kind that could only be associated with true love.

I've never done this with a woman without paying her in cash, he thought as he debated whether to proceed or not. *I'm not sure what to do. She likes me and trusts me, or at least I think she does, but I don't want to do the wrong thing. Those other women,* he continued silently, *let me do whatever I wanted because I was paying them, or they told me exactly what they wanted me to do. They were never shy with their words, not shy at all. This is so different.*

Despite her increasingly bold behavior over the last half hour, he noticed Lihua's face displayed an uncertainty about the direction their interlude was headed.

Darik continued to question himself as their hands, working in unison, slowly pulled up her dress, raising it to her belly. His fingers and hers, clasped together, slid over the center of her thighs for an instant, and she gasped as he pulled his hand away just as she leaned back and placed her hand on the front of his denims and touched the bulging material in a teasing manner that caused him to feel lightheaded.

Lihua's breathing changed and her heart raced like the wind as his fingers began to rest against a part of her body only she had touched prior to this moment.

Although neither wanted to stop, both seemed to be aware that they were entering into something from which they would have no recourse. Darik, in particular, wanted to be sure that he was not taking advantage of the young woman and thought he should slow down, if only briefly.

As though perfectly choreographed, they slowly separated their lips, never taking their eyes off one another, and he placed the carving tool and the birdhouse back into the satchel.

"I have to let you down from the saddle while I attach the birdhouse to the tree. Is that all right? It'll just take a few minutes, and then you can get back up here if you'd like."

"Understand."

As Darik dismounted he realized that he wanted to take her right then, all of her, and that the birdhouse could wait. He held her with both hands as they stood face to face with their bodies pressed together. Although Darik was more than a foot taller than Lihua, their torsos fit together like two perfectly designed embossments.

They said nothing.

She stroked Darik in an oval pattern with feather-like pressure, her fingers tracing every detail of his face. Her caress reminded him of the first time he touched a bolt of silk in a shop in Bucharest long ago with his grandparents. He placed his lips on her neck, sliding them up and down, nibbling her delicate skin, inhaling her jasmine fragrance.

Darik felt the rapid rising and lowering of her chest, something he suspected she would not think was ladylike, but it felt as though she was surrendering to the moment.

Lihua took the reins from his hand, tied them to a nearby bush and led Darik a few yards away to a small patch of buffalo grass the size of two picnic blankets. She began unbuttoning her blouse, starting at her waistline. He stared in silence. When her hands reached the top button and she pushed the blouse off her shoulders, he sighed, stepped forward, placed his hands on the sides of her breasts and caressed both nipples, leaning his head down so he could kiss the nape of her neck.

He removed his hat, tossed it to the ground, and then began unsnapping his shirt. She appeared unsure of what to do next and stood motionless.

Then, without either saying another word, she reached around to the back of her dress and fiddled with the largest button until the dress fell to the ground. She picked it up, folded it carefully and handed it to him. "Please put with blouse," she whispered. Darik complied.

Her undergarments were as white as the whitest clouds Darik could imagine, somewhat translucent in a way that exaggerated every feature of her body. He gasped softly, instinctively, as his eyes scanned her from head to toe. He was mesmerized by the dramatic contrast between the white garments, her jet black hair, and her amber colored skin. She was tiny, certainly in comparison to most of the women he had been with at the brothel, yet he was entranced by her enticing shape which was much more that of a mature woman than he had anticipated.

She stepped forward and kissed him above his left breast. She reached her arms around him and began rubbing his back with her silk-like hands. Her head was pressed against his ribs as her hands slid down to his back and came to rest on his buttocks. His hands replicated her movements and he gently squeezed her hips, lifting her up high enough for their lips to meet. He imagined that her mind was racing as much as his own, but he also sensed that she must have been feeling enough trust in him to be doing this of her own accord.

"I'm yours if you want me," he whispered.

"I do," she replied.

With one hand he undid the small blanket roll strapped onto the back of his saddle, tossed it down the ground, and then used his foot to spread it out. He lowered her to a standing position, and they removed the remainder of their clothing.

He had a hunch that the battle waging between her innate shyness and their total nudity was disturbing her, so he moved deliberately as he lowered her to the blanket and began stroking her body with feather-like pressure. He wondered if she was trying to explain to herself what was taking place.

They rolled around the blanket slowly, kissing passionately, their bodies linked together so tightly that neither was able to breathe without a slight stammer. There was no reference to time, space, or the potential ramifications of two young adults, fundamentally strangers, making love. The concept of sinning or the consideration of pregnancy did not enter into their thoughts. He felt levitated, free from gravity, and soon they were engaged in intercourse, doing what he thought and hoped would be the first of an infinite amount of lovemaking with her.

As his fingers roamed her body, her breathing became erratic. Her eyes opened wide enough to see every detail of Darik's face before he watched them slowly roll back ever so slightly as bliss overtook her.

"This is gift I share with you. No one else. You. Forever."

He smiled with such ferociousness that his jaw began to ache as she stroked his erection, something prior to this moment she never imagined happening and something he had never expected to be so overwhelming.

"I won't lie to you right now or ever again," he said while staring into her eyes, "I've been with other women, more than I'd admit to anyone else, but I had no idea what love like this would feel like. No idea. I love you, Lihua, and I will love you as long as we're alive. No," he laughed, "even beyond that."

She moved her legs apart and guided him back into her. "What call these feelings? What English word?"

"Heaven. I call it heaven. To me this is heaven. Do you know heaven?"

"When die? That heaven?"

He laughed. "No, when alive. To me heaven is the place that most of us dream about one way or the other our entire lives. It's different for each of us, and I think it's a place beyond words," he continued as his slow, shallow thrusts caused small tears to form in her eyes.

She whispered, "Something change. Did not believe pain would be so good with love. Good pain. Not really pain. Not know what it is. But good."

The tempo of his lower body's movements increased as her stared into Lihua's euphoric expression. He shouted with pleasure while her soft words of joy blended with the small tears filling her eyes, all of this in perfect synchrony as their lovemaking led to her first orgasm and, for Darik, the most intense of his life. It felt to him as though an earthquake was rocking the ground beneath the blanket.

They remained motionless for a few minutes before Darik looked up and noticed the afternoon sun was less than two hours from setting. He stood up slowly and extended his hand to help her to her feet. They embraced and he moved behind her, slowly and deliberately, and re-entered her. She melted in his grasp as her breathing seemed to come to a halt. Following one final deep kiss, he withdrew from her body.

Lihua remained silent and seemed to be swimming in a myriad of wild sensations when she said, "Must go. Late. Cannot be seen with you. Mrs. Brown not approve. Go back to ranch before too late. Come back another day."

Darik smiled. "Missy, we have just enough time to mount the birdhouse to the tree. Let's not rush. Lihua, please, I want this afternoon to last forever and to make sure everything else we do from now on is as perfect."

They dressed. Hand-in-hand with Lihua, he led the horse back to the stand of cottonwoods.

Before Darik remounted his horse, he pulled out a small hand drill from the satchel. Through the front opening of the hollowed out birdhouse, he made three holes that penetrated its back wall. The wood was nearly an inch thick and, even with a sharp drill bit, he had to push it forcefully through the back wall of the birdhouse as it rested on the ground.

He reached into the satchel once more and took out three long screws, a narrow-handled screwdriver with a long shaft, and a wooden-handled awl. He asked Lihua to hold the screws and screwdriver while he remounted the horse, turned a little to the side, and punched three starter holes into the tree trunk, one for each screw.

The young cottonwood's trunk was soft. The tip of the awl penetrated deeply enough for him to then twist the first few threads of one of the screws into the wood before withdrawing it with his fingers. He was careful not to fall from his precarious position on the saddle. Lihua handed him the birdhouse and screwdriver. He raised the birdhouse to the height of his rib cage as he sat atop the horse and then pushed the first long screw through the birdhouse's front opening and into the uppermost hole he had drilled through its back.

He placed the screwdriver into the recessed slot on the hand-forged screw and pressed it and the birdhouse against the tree trunk and began turning the screw head at a carefully measured pace. It took only a few seconds to drive the screw into its final position deep into the tree trunk. He eyeballed the birdhouse, leveled it to his satisfaction, and then pushed the second screw into place, pressed and turned it with the screwdriver until it, too, was firmly in position. He completed the same task with the third screw. He handed the screwdriver back to Lihua and pressed his hands against the birdhouse to try and wiggle it to check its stability. It felt locked in place.

He dismounted. They stepped back three feet and looked at one another without kissing. They moved back farther, nodded in agreement about the positioning of the birdhouse, again without kissing. He lifted her back atop the saddle and then remounted himself. Sitting behind Lihua, he pressed his loins against the back of her body, a body that now belonged to a woman who had experienced lovemaking for the first time.

Darik coaxed the horse back another few feet so he and Lihua could see the birdhouse from several angles. He guided the horse to the side of the cottonwood for a final look.

They nodded at one another. She looked at him and leaned towards his mouth and kissed him softly. "Forever."

He smiled. "Forever."

"Our secret. Forever," she said. "No one must know. Our place. Our birdhouse. Our tree."

"Yes, our secret place," he replied. "Our tree. Our birdhouse. Our hearts."

Darik knew that the heart was a functional organ of the body, and he also knew that the heart she referred to while they made love was at the core of their souls. It was something that until this very afternoon he had doubted was real, and he now wondered about its configuration, its timing, and its meaning to their lives.

They rode back to the sunflower field without exchanging another word, soon arriving where he saw her for the first time weeks earlier. In a sense, it felt as though he was revisiting the most important moment of his life, a moment that would be forever etched into his soul.

"Do not understand what I feel," she commented while looking into his eyes as he dismounted and then assisted her down. "But this I want. You I want. I not know such things exist. Not know birdhouses carved from inside out. Not know kisses from inside out. Not know heart pounding from inside out. This I want. Forever."

He smiled. "We'll learn about each other. We'll carve birdhouses together. I'll teach you the secrets. And we'll find a way to be together."

She smiled. "Meet in few days? Here?"

"Yes. Three days from now. Same time. Just before supper on Saturday. Can you be here?"

"Yes. Forever here for you."

She walked over the knoll leading toward Mrs. Brown's large summer home as Darik began his ride back to the Eagle Trail Ranch where he thought he would now begin a lifetime of carving birdhouses for Lihua.

CHAPTER 10
Reconsideration

His thoughts returned to his childhood in Romania during his ride to the ranch. Although he had no logical explanation for this bout of sentimentality, something inside told him that it was crucial to refresh his memory and revisit the feelings he had prior to settling in Colorado.

Damn, he thought while soaking in the beauty of the foothills to his right as his hour-long ride to Eagle Trail commenced, *it seems like a lifetime ago that I was just thirteen and celebrating my bar mitzvah with my grandparents, and that was only two months before I finally made it from Bucharest to Constanta and got on a ship and headed to America. My god, just getting all the way to Constanta with Grandfather driving his little wagon took days and days. I felt badly that he had to ride all the way back to the farm by himself, but he told me that knowing I was heading to America was the proudest moment of his life. He told me to never forget who I was and to always look forward and to always keep my eye on the path of the sun until I found what I was looking for. He and Grandmother couldn't have ever imagined all that's happened to me during this adventure.*

Darik had grown up on his grandparents' small farm a short distance from Bucharest. His family were among the few remaining Jews in the area, and, like all the rest of them, they had to keep their religious practices as invisible as possible due to widespread anti-Semitism throughout their homeland in the years leading up to Darik's departure. Most Jews had fled the Bucharest area over the prior decade; some emigrating to America, some to Canada, some to other countries in Europe, and even some to South Africa. Darik's grandparents, however, felt an inseparable connection to their homeland, their farm, and the surrounding forests, and those factors prevented them from ever leaving.

Darik's determination to discover a brighter, more creative future led him to America although the concept of creativity was not something he discussed with anyone other than his grandparents and the old wise woman in their village. Following the nine-day wagon trip to Constanta and twenty-three additional days on two separate sailing vessels traversing the Mediterranean, port by port through Greece, Italy and Portugal, and then across the Atlantic to New York, he was unsure what would be his final destination on the American mainland. However, during the transatlantic portion of the trip, he heard countless stories about the American Wild West from fellow travelers. It was then he decided to head across the country to this exciting region if he could find odd jobs during the three-month trek on a wagon train that would eventually land him in Denver, a bustling cattle town where the discovery of gold had occurred only a few years prior to his arrival.

Grandfather would have been pleased that I was able to save the small amount of money he gave me when the trip began, and it wasn't because I was frugal. No, it was because I was able to work my way across America on the wagon train. Everything he taught me about hard work, farming, and carpentry paid off.

Most people didn't think a boy my age could be so skilled at fixing things, including repairing the Conestoga wagons, but it was like going to school and getting paid for it, he mused as he made it halfway back to Eagle Trail within thirty minutes.

Carving wood was never limited to being a hobby for Darik, nor was it for his grandfather, the man who introduced him to woodworking and shared so many of his insights. Woodworking, even more than farming, reflected a philosophy about life and living that connected both of them to nature, and it was an essential ingredient in them both embracing a life filled with beauty whether they were farming or carving wood.

First and foremost, his grandfather was a farmer, a successful one by local standards, but more importantly he was a skilled artisan and man of nature who taught his grandson every detail of his relationship with wildlife, the trees, the forests, the cutting of wood, and an uncanny knowledge of how to sculpt birdhouses from solid blocks of wood rather than constructing them from individual wooden panels cut from larger planks.

From age five through nine, once his chores on the farm were completed, Darik spent each evening with his grandfather sitting between an oversized pair of brass kerosene lamps working on his carvings, learning all he could about sculpting birdhouses, eventually refining his skills through trial and error as he grew older.

His grandfather shared secret after secret about woodworking and the mystical art of transforming wooden blocks into carved birdhouses. By age eleven, two years before he left for America, Darik had a growing reputation in the Romanian countryside as an artisan in his own right. He was known a young master carver with wizard-like woodworking skills unlike anyone in the region including the elders.

Some considered Darik to be a prodigy. Others, particularly those jealous of his youthful competency, considered him precocious because of his supreme self-confidence. However, Darik, much in the same manner as his grandfather, paid little attention to how others viewed him or his woodworking skills.

The old woman, Baba, the crone who lived near his grandparents' farm, was reputed to possess the mystical knowledge of alchemy and various ancient healing methods. She advised Darik's grandfather that the boy's birdhouses would someday be recognized as the finest in the land once he set sail on his life adventure. His grandfather never imagined that Darik would actually set sail for America at age thirteen to pursue the next chapter of his life, but he trusted the crone's wisdom and never balked at Darik's decision to leave Romania.

Darik's finely detailed birdhouses were the most beautiful works of art the old woman had ever seen. They were impervious to breakage and the ravages of weather. But to her, their true power was in their innate capacity to serve as energetic vortices far beyond the understanding of most people. She had noticed that no matter where Darik's birdhouses were displayed—in shops, yards, or inside homes in Bucharest where many ended up—people were drawn to them as though a magnet was pulling them in.

Darik's grandfather had no formal education beyond rudimentary Talmudic studies done in secret during his own childhood. He had limited exposure to the modern science of the times. And while he had no idea what the old crone meant about energy or vortices, he believed in magic and remained devoted to the mysterious, ritualistic ways of the old world.

Darik's grandfather had witnessed the old woman's alchemy at work frequently during the fifty years they knew one another. He trusted her with blind faith, especially when it came to foretelling the future or interpreting his own lucid dreams, the details of which he had never shared with anyone else.

Darik thought back to how his grandfather would help him decipher his dreams. *That old Baba woman and Grandfather would sit me down in our kitchen and ask me about each detail of my night visions, whatever I could remember. It was as though I had read them from a book and could recount them perfectly. They helped me unravel the meaning of the stories and images in ways I couldn't have done for myself. They taught me to look so much deeper within myself no matter what I was doing—awake, asleep, or in my dreams,* he concluded. In the distance he could see the large windmill at Eagle Trail Ranch towering above the barn and large corral.

As a result of working so intently with his grandfather, Darik, a natural listener even at an early age, had become proficient in grasping the deeper meaning of his night dreams and the daydreams he experienced frequently during his awakened hours. Although he never was able to explain the relationship between his curiosity about dreams and his love affair with trees, the forests, and the carving of birdhouses, he always sensed that he was some sort of conduit that connected the dreams and the birdhouses together.

However, once Darik embarked on his journey to America, he began paying less attention to the disciplined practices his grandfather and Baba had taught him, both about carving and about delving into the power and meaning of his dreams. By the time his travels across the North American continent by wagon train concluded six months later when he arrived in Denver in 1870, the thirteen-year-old was completely caught up in the excitement of what was an endless supply of storybook adventures taking place each day in and around Denver, a crude and uncivilized gold mining town at its inception a decade earlier. As Derik examined his options in Denver, he ruled out anything to do with mining and instead sought out work at one of the immense farms or ranches in the general vicinity because of the amount of work he had experienced on his grandfather's farm. It turned out that by knocking on a few doors, including the marshal's office, he learned that one of the largest ranches in Louviers, Double Eagle Ranch, located twenty miles south of Denver, had an opening for a young man who could take on basic chores that most ranch hands were not apt to do. The next morning after sleeping on a stack of hay at one of the many livery stables in town, Darik grabbed his belongings and spent the next six hours walking to the ranch. After his arrival and a brief discussion with the ranch foreman, Darik was hired.

As he attempted to fit into the cowboy mindset over the next several years at Double Eagle, many of the cultural traditions of his family and of Romania began to diminish in their importance without him noticing. By the time Darik celebrated his seventeenth birthday four years later, he was a skilled horseman and, as a result of being treated to the Louviers' brothel by his fellow ranch hands, he was no longer a virgin. Losing that final vestige of his youth and finally enjoying the companionship of women, albeit for money, Darik's focus shifted from carving birdhouses in his spare time at the ranch to saving enough money to make the one-hour horseback ride twice each month to enjoy the pleasures of the whorehouse.

Over time as the novelty wore off of having sex with a different woman each subsequent visit, he began to treat the women as friends because of his own affable nature. As a result, he re-adjusted his life at the ranch and reaffirmed his commitment to carving birdhouses with increased skill and creativity. With his confidence growing and facial hair requiring him to shave once a month, Darik vigorously pursued the various interests that a young cowboy in his mid-twenties found appealing, as well as having sex as often as the money in his pocket would allow.

The women at the brothel enjoyed his naiveté and youthful appearance, which were in contrast to the strikingly mature way he told stories about his life in Romania as well as his tall tales about forests, trees, and carving birdhouses. He gifted numerous birdhouses to these working women in Louviers over the next half-dozen years although he was a paying client, unquestionably so. But it did not take long for him to realize there were never any free sessions at the brothel. He was viewed as a refreshing change of pace for the prostitutes compared to the brothel's predominant audience of cowboys and farmers, and he was often the topic of parlor room discussions because of his endless desire to bring pleasure to each of them, at least that is what he thought he was doing. What they liked most about the young cowboy was his relentless energy and an eagerness to learn all the lessons about sex and women that they were willing to share with him. However, even they recognized that there existed a shallow pit of emotional emptiness and fierceness in Darik that was far stronger than what they often experienced with their cowboy clients, and he was outspoken in the fierce way he expressed his need for both solitude and freedom.

Throughout this period of sexual maturation, Darik became aware that he had two palettes from which to pursue his drive as an artist, at least when he was not paying for sex. One was carving birdhouses, and in a sense the other was the crafting of his dreams, something he realized he could accomplish and felt he could control each night or, at the very least, remain lucid enough to knowingly participate in these dreamscapes. Yet even as his carving skills grew exponentially over the years, his lifelong ability to communicate with the trees in the forest got rusty, and he began taking this innate skill for granted, often ignoring the specifics of what was being told to him by the trees.

In the same way some artists worked exclusively with oil paints and some worked with watercolors, each making his or her own media from local flowers, leaves, roots, soft twigs, bark and berries, even before he left for America, Darik understood wood and knew as much about forests as many of the scholars at the university in nearby Bucharest, those who learned from books, lectures, in laboratories, or from field experience. None could match the boy's knowledge about this subject. Although he did not have the polished vocabulary to explain his insights, he had always sensed that in a mysterious sort of way the fibers in trees were similar to the way his mind bridged dreams together and how these nighttime adventures could be applied to his life and the successes and disappointments he would face during his many journeys.

Darik's grandfather had taught him to communicate with each tree in the section of forest where they did most of their gathering. As a result, Darik understood the soul of the wood as though it was purposefully sharing its deepest secrets with him. His grandfather realized that even he was not as attuned to the language of the trees as was his grandson. Wood seemed to converse with this boy who had a knack for listening to what the live trees, as well as the dead ones, had to say.

Darik believed that tree rings did not simply define the age of trees but were the actual chapters to the sagas of the natural world that each tree kept housed within its fibrous structure, trunk, bark, leaves, and, most importantly, deep within its roots. It was only until such time that someone with Darik's sensitivity came along, which was not often, that his grandfather and the old crone believed the trees would share their insights. To them, each birdhouse Darik carved was a potential passageway, a conduit that would enable the boy to maneuver more effectively within the external world of tangible matter and would strengthen his focus on the internal world of the soul, spirit, and the energy that connects all things.

Hank Fisher

The Conestoga wagon moved at a dangerously high rate of speed as it hurdled the crevice separating two immense canyon walls, landing as softly as a feather on the far side, adjacent to acres of tulips, each of which had a multi-colored sunflower rising from within the center of its petals. The fields vibrated as a steady breeze raked the myriad of colors packed together as densely as grass. He turned to see who or what was moaning beneath the canvas tarp covering the storage area in the rear of the wagon that was now moving without a horse, mule, or oxen doing the pulling. A beautiful woman with crimson colored hair was kneeling above a grizzled man older than his grandfather. She was humming an eerie harp-like sound common only to angels who had visited his dreams over the years, a sonorous melody combining bliss and rapture. Her nakedness was natural and she displayed complete satisfaction as the man's tongue caressed the valley between her legs. Gunshots in the distance caused the woman to suddenly turn, lift her body from the old man, and float away from his grasp as she evaporated into the ethos. The old man stood up momentarily, looked for her without success, and as tears poured from his fiery red eyes, gently placed his face into the pile of blankets upon which the two had been entangled in lust. The image of the woman's large eyes seemed to be everywhere—in the clouds, in the nearby trees and fields of tulips that stretched into the horizon.

CHAPTER 11
Inferno

On Saturday, the third day since he made love with Lihua and attached her birdhouse to the cottonwood sapling near the north bank of Bear Creek, Darik rode from the ranch back to the sunflower field for their rendezvous. In the distance he saw a thread of black smoke rising over the northwestern hills a mile from his destination.

That's not far enough east for the foundry along the Platte," he thought to himself. *And the smoke's not the right color or odor. That's wood burning and not the smell of molten metals.*

He saw flames as he approached the plateau several hundred yards south of Lihua's sunflower field and was shocked to see Mrs. Brown's large three-story brick Victorian adorned with ornate ironwork and small sculptures inundated in flames.

A handful of Mrs. Brown's staff had formed a fire brigade and were passing buckets of water at a frenetic pace to several men at the front who were throwing it onto the burning house, but their efforts were having no effect on the blaze. The intense heat forced the men to back away from the structure while Darik, still on horseback, remained twenty yards away. His carpentry experience convinced him that the house was beyond saving and would be nothing more than a pile of ash and glowing embers within minutes.

He dismounted and approached several people who were embracing one another as tears streamed down their soot-covered faces and cries of grief filled the air. He saw a bejeweled, well-dressed woman he assumed was Mrs. Brown, kneeling alone, wailing in anguish.

He had never met Mrs. Brown, but she was well known throughout the region. He tied off his horse, walked over to her and asked, "Is there anything I can do to help?"

She had never seen him before, but by her stern expression he sensed she was in shock and rejected his offer silently. She was then joined by an elderly Chinese woman who appeared to be a housekeeper. The two women hugged one another as they stood over a large piece of scorched burlap. Darik had seen death in Romania in his small village, death from old age, disease, and farm injuries, but never from a fire, at least none he could remember. A strong, sudden gust of wind blew the burlap off the victim.

His mind exploded in terror and his breathing stopped momentarily as he choked from the pungent odor of burnt flesh mixed with an instantaneous shock that consumed him. He quaked in pain, fell to his knees, and lowered his head into his palms. A dark cloud of impenetrable silence replaced the sounds of the roaring flames as the building collapsed upon itself and he stared at the lifeless body of what had once been a young woman from China, Lihua, whose beautiful face was severely burned and hardly recognizable. Rather than attempting to speak again with Mrs. Brown, he stood, walked back to his horse, remounted and rode away in silence.

Hank Fisher

Flying within a large cast of falcons numbering in the hundreds, he was the only pure white one and was leading the group as its density was so great that to those looking up from a small village below it appeared to be a semi-translucent cloud passing overhead. The birds nearest to him were speaking in Romanian, telling of past times when prey was more available and the nesting process was not undermined by heavy foresting. To the rear of his tail feathers, he overhead a conversation in English between two female falcons complaining that neither trusted their mates insofar as being in the nest of another female falcon when the mate was supposed to be gathering food for the family. Undeterred, but bored with the conversation, he dove down to a fishing boat bouncing around in heavy seas that appeared out of nowhere, landing in the crow's nest, undetected by crew members. He recognized the captain. It was Mulroony, his boss from the ranch, and the second mate was Silvano. They were arguing about Darik—the boss asking what had become of the young man—Silvano commenting that the last anyone had seen Darik he was having sex with two women at the brothel in Louviers but that he had disappeared after thinking he had fallen in love with both of them. Having heard enough, the white falcon flew away from the crow's nest in the opposite direction of the other falcons that were now beyond sight. The falcon was unsteady in flight, eventually coming to rest on a boulder-encased cauldron atop a mountain more than seventy-five miles south of the ranch, a peak that stood out against the plains like Mount Olympus. As he approached the glowing rocks and lava spewing into the air, he saw the silhouette of a young woman whose clothing was entirely transparent. The bird of prey dove down to see if the woman was Lihua, but she vanished into thin air before he could land.

CHAPTER 12
Exodus

Darik traveled slowly after he rode away from Mrs. Brown's in a meandering pattern toward the ranch, seemingly without any purpose, not seeing anyone on the side trails, never dismounting, and only stopping alongside an irrigation ditch to water his horse.

His initial thought was to inform Mulroony and Silvano about the fire as well as to share his brief love story about Lihua, but instead he chose not to say a word to anyone about his grief, even these men who guided him from boyhood to manhood.

For the first time he could remember, thoughts about his own childhood in Romania and his confusion about his parents' absence from his life crossed his mind. He loved his grandparents but never understood, nor had he asked them in specific terms why it was they raised him and why his parents were never a part of his life. He knew both his parents had died, but beyond that basic fact, he avoided the subject and never sought an explanation nor did his grandparents broach the subject.

Looking back on his childhood, he was unsure if he had failed to comprehend what his grandparents might have told him about the death of his parents when he was only an infant, and he now wondered if he had simply forgotten the details. He had great love and respect for his grandparents and learned to balance the nurturing they provided at the farm with his innate desire to travel, to explore new things, and to come to terms with the solitary journey he began at thirteen when he left Romania.

It was three in the afternoon when he reached the ranch. Instead of entering through the main gate on the east side of the property which would have taken him past Mulroony's house, he circled to the southwest, quietly riding up to the bunkhouse he and the other ranch hands called their home. The building appeared empty.

He tied off his horse and entered the bedroom where his few personal belongings were stored in the mid-sized leather-covered trunk he brought with him from Romania years earlier. He opened it and carefully put into it his satchel of tools, three shirts, long johns, one pair of heavy denims, and a few other items he wanted for the journey about to begin. He closed the trunk, sat down by the small table in the corner of the room, and wrote a simple note to Mulroony and Silvano:

> *Dear Boss and Silvano,*
> *Time to leave. Will explain someday.*
> *Thank you for everything.*
> *Darik*

He carried the small trunk out to his horse, attached it to his saddlebag, and headed south by southeast toward Castle Rock.

He arrived at Lynetta's property at sundown, five hours after he left the ranch. He did not announce his arrival. Several kerosene lamps in Lynetta's home were visible as he dismounted and led his horse to the barn. He removed the bridle, saddle and blanket, brushed the animal for a shorter time than usual, set out a bucket of water, some oats and alfalfa, and spread out a blanket for himself atop a six-inch layer of hay in the next stall. He laid down, never removing his clothing or boots, and fell asleep within seconds. He awakened at dawn thoroughly exhausted from the events of the past twelve hours. He stared at the ceiling and tried to imagine what his scattered dreams had been trying to tell him.

The barn door opened. He smiled as Lynetta approached. She was carrying a small tray with a cup of steaming coffee and a plate of cooked eggs.

"We heard you ride up last night, Darik, but when you didn't come into the house we knew something terrible had happened. Don't explain anything right now. Not a word. You need to eat. Sometime, when you're ready and if you have a mind to, let me know why you're here. We both love you, Ingrid and me, so whatever it is, I'm glad you realize we're family."

He stood up and took the tray from Lynetta, set it down on the ground, and gave the woman an embrace that nearly took the wind out of her.

"I just need to be here right now."

"Looks like," she replied.

"Please don't say nothin' to Ingrid just yet. Okay?"

"Honey, she sat up most the night. That girl loves you in ways you can't imagine and she's worried sick. When the time's right, tell her whatever it is you need to say. Deal?"

"Yep. Deal."

Two days passed before Darik spoke to Ingrid. Finally, after finishing one of Lynetta's suppers out in the barn, his temporary sanctuary, he walked toward the hot springs twenty yards past the barn and noticed that Ingrid was soaking. A dense, foggy cloud hovered over the water, providing ample privacy.

"I need to explain something to you," he said.

"Are you sure?" she asked.

He nodded and sat down a several feet from the edge of the mist-covered spring so as not to violate her privacy. For more than an hour, he detailed his encounters with Lihua, from their first meeting to the fire at Mrs. Brown's home. He left out nothing. He felt Ingrid's genuine concern and recognized that she was offering a type of intimate friendship he had never experienced with anyone, let alone a woman.

Days passed into weeks and into several months. By early November, Darik found himself wrapped up in the world Lynetta had created for herself and Ingrid to such a degree that he decided he would spend his life with the two women—one as his friend and muse, the other as his wife.

Lynetta, without meaning to, took on much the same role in his life as Baba had in Romania, as his guide and teacher, but the ever-increasing connection with Ingrid became so soothing, supportive, and tender for Darik that marriage felt like a natural and logical progression, and it would provide a life in which he could immerse himself in a calmness that was much to his liking. He recognized his sexual attraction to Ingrid was far different from what he had felt about Lihua, yet while he and Ingrid were passionate lovers, they pursued their shared life in a safe and controlled manner. As the months and years passed, Darik convinced himself that the kind of wild sexual abandon he once felt with Lihua was probably more of a mirage, some sort of dreamlike fantasy, and that in the real world he would be satisfied with what Ingrid and he could create together.

The first major change after the marriage was in their location. Lynetta, tired of living in Castle Rock after twenty-five years, decided to relocate the family she'd assembled piece by piece just across the New Mexico border into a small, somewhat primitive village she had learned about from travelers over the years, a place called Tejada that was nestled near the foothills fronting the vast mountains of the Sangre de Cristos.

Despite being asked frequently by Ingrid and Lynetta to carve new birdhouses after they settled in Tejada, Darik denied their requests. He believed his tools were put away permanently and that he would avoid carving from then on. Memories of Lihua, especially engraving their names atop the roof of her birdhouse the day they made love so passionately, were relentless although as time passed he was able to quell those images even though he knew both Ingrid and Lynetta sensed the turmoil that still simmered within him. Instead of carving, he immersed himself in learning what he could from Lynetta about the healing power of local flowers and plant life, how to prepare natural medicines, and the use of crystals and minerals, as he built increasing familiarity with the alchemy she utilized that was somewhat similar to what he had witnessed from Baba in Romania.

MARCH 1888

CHAPTER 13
Revival

The most notable change in Darik's life occurred at the conclusion of his first year of marriage, several months after arriving in Tejada, when Ingrid gave birth to their daughter, Theresa. At the moment he held his daughter in his arms seconds after Lynetta used her midwifing skills to assist in the delivery, he found himself feeling like an adult for the first time, immensely hopeful about life in ways that took him by surprise. Theresa's birth was confirmation that he belonged to a family of his own, something he had not experienced fully since he left Romania.

Theresa and Ingrid became inseparable focal points in an intense love he never anticipated would be part of his life after Lihua's death. It was the love of a husband for his wife and that of a father for his daughter, love that grew with increasing depth over the next three years until Ingrid suddenly took seriously ill, eventually dying five months later. Day in and day out, he mourned what he accepted would soon be his wife's death. For Lynetta, however, the elongated grieving process she experienced was defined in large part by a wavering sense of guilt as she questioned her judgment about leaving the healing waters flowing through her property in Castle Rock five years earlier. Although her pragmatic side remained dominant in how she observed Ingrid's illness and death, her more mystical side had her questioning whether or not the conditions they experienced after arriving in Tejada played a role in the young woman's death. Nonetheless, she also understood that the pathways defining one's fate and one's destiny, concepts and journeys she saw as related but different from one another, would never provide her or Darik with reliable explanations about the reasons for Ingrid's passing, something they both recognized as part of the natural cycle of life that humans could not control.

* * *

Darik stood at the graveside with Theresa as two local men lowered Ingrid's casket into the ground in the Tejada cemetery. Theresa, approaching her fourth birthday, had blonde hair identical to her late mother's and the sapphire blue eyes of her father. Lynetta's arm was wrapped around Darik's shoulder as tears streamed from her eyes for the first time Darik could recall.

Theresa, sobbing, threw a handful of sunflowers and a beautiful ristra atop the casket as it reached the bottom of the grave. Darik shoveled red clay soil onto the casket. After a dozen tosses, Lynetta took the shovel from his shaky hands and threw more of Tejada's iron-rich soil onto the casket. Not to be left out, Theresa, unable to lift the shovel, kneeled down and grabbed a handful of the red soil and threw it onto her mother's casket.

Nearly five years with Ingrid had brought Darik a sense of peace. He experienced new levels of self-awareness that were buoyed by marriage and the birth of his daughter once he, Ingrid, and Lynetta resettled on a rancho southwest of Tejada, less than a mile from a steep trail that led to what locals called Tejada

Junction near a horse path that crossed one of the shallowest portions of the Rio Concho Canyon.

In the time since Darik rode away from Mulroony's ranch the afternoon of the destruction of Mrs. Brown's home, he had tried to be a dependable husband and father. His initial move into the barn adjacent to Lynetta's apothecary gave him the opportunity to begin grieving and to tend his broken heart, while secondarily giving him enough time to construct a new barn with sleeping quarters she could rent by the night to travelers since there were no hotels near Castle Rock.

Darik sat by the fire pit he built on the far side the hacienda after returning from the funeral. He stared into the embers for an hour without uttering a sound, occasionally looking up into the Milky Way which seemed within reach most nights in this high altitude village in the Sangre de Cristo Mountains.

"Been more than four years since I sold the store in Castle Rock," Lynetta said as she approached him holding a cup of coffee. "I moved down here with you and Ingrid to start over, for all of us to start over, and then this heavenly child arrived. You know something, Darik, the soul of the Sangre de Cristos is more powerful than anything I'd ever imagined. It's strange, I suppose," she continued, "that Lihua's death became the threshold for you and Ingrid to begin anew. That terrible loss allowed you and my niece to discover this wonderful love and to create your greatest masterpiece, Theresa. What's next? You look so lost. I'll always be this child's grandmother, nothing will change that, and will always be your friend, but what do you want for yourself?"

He gazed at her, his own swollen eyes leaking salty tears. "I have no clue. None at all. I'm Theresa's father, but it feels like I'm in quicksand and there's nothing to keep me from sinking. Is that normal? Is this how my life is supposed to be?"

"Nobody's life's normal, son. Nobody's. I know that sounds like bullshit from some old lady, something I'm saying to keep you from blowing your brains out. But it's the truth. I began life in Holland, landed in New York not knowing a word of English as a young girl in what seems like a lifetime ago. Then I traveled to Ohio where my parents decided to settle and then came to Colorado with my brother and his wife who only stayed a year before they left for Oregon. Is this the story of my life as I'd have written it? Who knows? None of us really knows our destiny any more than we know the fates that might challenge us. In fact, I'm not sure anything was ever supposed to be one way or the other. I think we're in constant motion.

"Is the story of that old Ute medicine man's life in Castle Rock, the man who taught me about Ute prayer trees and the magical hot springs behind the store, exactly as he or his forefathers would have believed possible before the whites came to America and stole their land? No, but it's the life he lived. Same thing for Theresa. Same thing for you. If Lihua hadn't died and your sorrow hadn't led you back to Castle Rock and Ingrid, there wouldn't have been Theresa, at least not this version."

"So is it all luck?" he asked. "Is my story just a wild ride in a buckboard on a steep road leading into a ravine…over and over again?"

"Could be. I don't really know. But as much as I love you, your self-pity is short-sighted. In some ways, I suppose, it's pretty much the case for everyone else too—tragedy mixed with joy. So don't think you're the only person who's had these kinds of down times. You know better than most folks that sometimes you suddenly get struck by lightning and walk away from it as a stronger and better person compared to just lying on the ground and dying. And if this journey on Earth were as simple as Theresa learning her ABCs and that was all there was to her life journey, then everyone you'd meet in your life would be happy as a lark.

And we know that ain't the case. Just not how things play out. Life's got its own path for each of us; at least that's what I believe. Not so much a plan as a path.

"Your job, my job, and now Theresa's is to travel the path no matter where it leads. It's what Ingrid did coming to Colorado and meeting you. And sure, her dying so young is cruel, no two ways about it. But that was the path her soul chose for her. I know it doesn't make sense. Not supposed to. But it ain't logic nor dumb luck that guides any of us. I think we're each supposed to grab hold of the reins and head toward our next destiny whether it's in this life or the next one, just as it might have been in a prior life. With all my heart, I believe this is all a grand illusion, at least most of it, although love itself is the most real thing in the universe.

"When that old medicine man and I smoked whatever it was he'd put in the pipe years ago when we'd sit by the hot springs and talk all night long, I went places that had nothing to do with what most people call reality. And maybe reality's the wrong word. What seems real might just be a dream. I'm not sure. Honestly, I don't know. I just trust my gut and know everything is going to work itself out one way or another. What's in our dreams—whether we smoke or drink something to escape this reality or we spend every spare minute praying to an invisible god in a church or a cave—might be more real than any of us ever imagined. It's not luck. This life, what you're experiencing right now, is just part of a meandering stream deep enough for the raft you're on whether it's high water, low water, or rapids leading to huge water falls beyond the next bend. Navigating your life, especially the unplanned parts, requires more skill than getting through the parts you've laid out. It's not much different from the way you carve birdhouses from the inside out and seem to know exactly how you want each one to look without some diagram to guide you."

"Did I ever tell you how much you remind me of my grandfather?" Darik commented in a melancholy tone. "You have a way of putting things together in ways I can grasp, at least most the time." He continued staring into her eyes with a curious, cautious expression. "It's always seemed that my birdhouses came out looking exactly how I imagined when I first grabbed hold of the wooden block."

"Seriously? No surprises ever? No knotholes? No flaws in the grain? No mistakes? You managed to carve perfectly each time you created a birdhouse?"

"No, of course not. Always some sort of problem when I carve. Always have to make small changes here and there. Little things. That's how it is. That's how my grandfather taught me to appreciate wood and the trees in the forest. He used to tell me that nothing in the forest was completely predictable other than the morning sun rising in the east and setting in the west.…"

"And," she interrupted, "you never know when lightning's gonna demolish a stand of trees or start a forest fire. Never know when biblical rains will cause a mudslide in that same burned forest before new scrub oak or saplings grow roots strong enough to hold the soil together. I don't know a lot of facts, Darik, I really don't. But the older I get, the more damn certain I am that nothing's exactly what it seems or I might have hoped it would be. That's what makes nearly everything worth exploring."

They returned to the hacienda. With Theresa's help, Lynetta slaughtered and plucked a chicken, chopped it into large pieces, and boiled it in a variety of herbs and flower tops picked from the field leading up to the small creek a short walk from the adobe home Darik constructed for his family.

Darik kissed his daughter goodnight after the meal was finished as she sat by the fire pit listening to one of Lynetta's stories. He walked over the small rise, dodging large yucca plants that dotted the property, and eventually reached the hot spring where he and Ingrid often soaked while discussing the life they created together in Tejada. He removed his clothing, lowered himself through the light fog that hovered over the water, and leaned his head back so he could watch shooting stars streak across the New Mexico sky.

"You need to leave," Lynetta said in a loving tone as she approached the hot springs a short time later. "It's plain to see that you need to get your head on straight. Theresa doesn't need to see you moping around like this. She doesn't. We both watched you suffer during Ingrid's illness. You got pretty low and that wasn't surprising. Ingrid's gone but you can't stay in this mood without hurting Theresa even if you don't mean to be doing it. She needs to see the wild-eyed craftsman and artist I know, the man she calls Papa, losing himself in his carving and demonstrating the enduring love he has for her with a smile, not the look of someone totally numb. Take yourself on a long horseback ride. Go somewhere else for a while and figure this out. I'll take care of her while you're gone; you know that. Figure out how you want to spend the rest of your life. I won't be around forever. Nobody is. You know that better than most."

"I've heard of a place in the Arizona Territory," he replied while adjusting his position in the water, "called Sedona. Supposed to be beautiful. Magical canyons and small mountains covered with rock formations with faces carved into them by nature. I'm told they look like humans and animals. It's a sacred place for the Indians. Not sure they have anything like the Ute prayer trees down there, but I'm sure they've got their own special totems and rituals. Supposed to be a great place for healing. Maybe I need to go there? I'll head that direction. Will Theresa hate me for leaving?"

"Hell, she's your daughter. Of course, she'll wonder why you're not here. But she can't hate you. Ever. That child adores you and deserves to have you here in one piece. She's so much like you, Darik. She sees the distant horizon with the eyes of a falcon, and she's got a hell of a lot of wisdom for a child. She's also got the soul of an ancient one. That's what it's felt like to me since the day she was born. And if she knew the right words, she'd tell you that her mother would want you to take some time for yourself.

"We're not going anywhere, and I can run the store without you just as easy as with you here. Saddle up and take those magical tools to Sedona. See what it's like. If it suits you, then stay until you get things in order. We'll be here living life until you return. And when you get back, we'll figure out the next steps on this journey."

JUNE 1888

Hank Fisher

Grayish white steam billowed upward in the shape of the letters of the alphabet, briefly forming the word FOREVER multiple times in varying sizes and shapes. "Forever" vanished as rapidly as it kept appearing while a black locomotive sped towards the setting sun, raising dust clouds as it chugged across the open desert plains. There were no tracks, no route to follow. Looking downward from the clouds, the soaring white falcon only saw the engine. There were no other cars attached to it. The black engine was alone in a solitary journey to a destination that could not be seen by the falcon. Abject silence enveloped everything. The engine was silent. The air through which the falcon flew was silent. And yet, even in the silence, the bird thought he heard a woman's voice saying, "Forever," repeatedly whispering, "Forever." The voice was soft and the source was not apparent. "Forever."

CHAPTER 14
Succubus

Nearly four months had passed since Darik's arrival in Sedona. Everything he imagined about this mystical area had proven true. There existed an omnipresent magnetism in and around Sedona, a powerful energetic force that seemed to capture every aspect of his being.

"Mr. Jacoby, did you finish up the corral fence?" a woman asked in a thick, sultry Spanish accent.

"End of the day, Mrs. Jaramillo, if that's okay. Had to ride halfway up that big hill to the south of your casita to find sturdy piñon pine timbers to drag back down. These should hold up for years. The trunks on the shorter ones were more brittle than I'd figured, so it took a while to cull through the stand to find what I needed for your fence. Sorry it's taking so long."

Brushing her flame red bangs from her forehead, the full-breasted woman pressed herself against his arm, patted him seductively on his buttocks and said, "No. Not long at all, Mr. Jacoby. You finished building the shed and tack room much faster than I'd anticipated, though I still wish we had large wooden planks to cover the inside walls. Once there's a mill in Sedona, you'll be able to build things the right way, that is, if you stay around here long enough."

"Adobe's great to work with," he replied as he tried to ignore her seductive tone. "You get awfully rough weather here, more so than what we get in Tejada, so the mud thatch for the roof is ideal. Snow's not all that rare in the winter around here 'though I don't know how often. Need to check with my friend Fierce Night Sky about winter weather. He knows more about Sedona than anyone else."

"So I've heard," she replied. "We only arrived here a few weeks before you. Only experienced the changing of late-spring to summer once, so I don't know what to expect for winter. Either way, my husband's broken leg makes it impossible for him to do any of the construction, so I'm indebted to you, especially in those special ways you and I have discovered.

"And in case that drunk son of a bitch husband of mine failed to mention it, you're welcome to stay on the property until you get some land of your own and build a casita. That's my personal invitation," she said while running her tongue over her lips. "Goes without saying that I enjoy having you around, especially after he's passed out. It's been quite nice, hasn't it?"

"Not likely I'll be staying here too much longer," he said sternly. "I've got a daughter in New Mexico. I'm missing the hell out of her. But thanks for the invitation. Our village is on the east side of the Rio Concho near a huge gorge where the Earth's split right in two. The river runs through it for miles when there's enough water, but that's not too often. I'll be heading back to Tejada before the leaves start falling whether there's been a snow or not. No real plan just yet."

She began walking back toward her husband who was sitting on the casita's front porch. His contorted facial expression conveyed disgust as he eavesdropped on yet another of his wife's conversations with the young man. His right leg was propped up on a bent willow chair for support and would remain wrapped in heavy plastered cloth for several more weeks to protect the bone he broke falling off their front porch during one of his drunken stupors. The older man, at least twenty years his wife's senior, cringed when he heard her sultry voice say, "I do hope you change your mind, Mr. Jacoby. I could really use a man like you to help me forget I ever agreed to settle in this god-forsaken place."

The penetrating expression in her green eyes told Darik that her personal needs would always exceed his carpentry skills.

"Anything I can do to help, just say so," he said, realizing that her insatiable sexual appetite would once again bring them together in his small bedroom in the barn later that evening. As had been the case since the day he met the Jaramillos, he found himself lusting for the buxom, highly manipulative woman. He knew that within a few hours they would be feasting upon one another's bodies without regard to Mr. Jaramillo, who, she claimed, would be passed out drunk as he was every time she lured Darik into her arms.

"That's what I hoped you'd say," Mrs. Jaramillo commented under her breath as she turned and walked past her injured husband and into the casita, wiggling her hips at Darik in what he thought was a preview of what would be presented to him in a few hours, as well as to further insult her husband. Using his cane for support, Mr. Jaramillo struggled to an upright position, limped through the open front door, and began another blistering verbal assault on his wife, all of it in Spanish. Darik's lack of Spanish fluency did not prevent him from understanding that the couple's turmoil had nothing to do with her husband's broken leg.

Darik spent the next two days preparing dozens of piñon pine poles to be cross members in the fence surrounding the new corral. This was mindless work for a skillful carpenter of Darik's caliber. Fence work was child's play compared to the precise mixing of Sedona soils with sand and water, shaping the muddy mixture into clay blocks that he dried in the hot sun and then preparing an adobe paste he applied in smooth layers over the cured blocks as he formed the exterior walls of the casita the last few months. The construction of the perimeter wall around the house and two other small structures, a large shed and a tack room attached to the small barn, was a perfect use of time as he continued sorting through his feelings about losing Ingrid to what Lynetta called *consumption*.

Darik recalled the helplessness Lynetta displayed on her weathered face as Ingrid, her niece, underwent a slow and tortuous death-by-inches process lasting four months. Nothing Lynetta could concoct in her kitchen nor provide in any other tangible ways, other than love itself, was of use. She requested that the tribal elders in Tejada have their shaman visit the dying young woman so he could use herbal remedies, incantations, blessings, and anything in his medicine bag that might ease Ingrid's pain. The shaman, a man considerably older than Darik and who spoke no English, made repeated visits, but his well-meaning efforts were no more productive than had been the painkilling liquid Lynetta made from nearby cactus plants and flowers, a thick and pungent mind-numbing gel that Ingrid sipped in increasingly large quantities to assuage the pain ravaging her young body.

* * *

Darik had brought his much needed carpentry skills to Sedona. He was rewarded handsomely for building a variety of small structures for the few white settlers in the area, people he mostly saw as interlopers in this sacred area where Palaki, *the Red House,* was etched into the Red Rock Canyon, the tribal home of the Sinagua people for countless generations.

As best as Darik could piece the Jaramillos' story together, they moved to Sedona to escape legal issues in El Paso and to open a small trading post for other settlers. Darik assumed Mrs. Jaramillo's decision to accompany her husband to Sedona was based entirely on her financial wants, and he doubted the couple would stay married for long. Darik sensed her disdain for the Red Rock Canyon and its native population and witnessed her abject disrespect for her husband each day. In some ways, possibly the coldness of her personality more than anything else, she reminded him of the prostitutes at the Louviers' brothel who first taught him about sex for money. As he looked back on his wilder and more youthful days, it seemed that those women were void of the kind of authentic emotions he had observed in Lihua and had experienced the past five years with Ingrid. He recalled a sense of emptiness that seemed inseparable from the women in Louviers, callous yet practical women, none of whom sought the permanent company of men, just the benefits gained from conducting commerce with them.

Through an open window leading into a luxuriously decorated bedroom in a castle, a female figure with shoulder length red hair floated between the sheer curtains until she shifted positions and began hovering over him. A strong perfume-like fragrance, possibly lilac, filled his senses as the naked woman's eyes conveyed a lust for him that removed all resistance from his body. Her head was tipped to one side as her lips engulfed his erect penis while her eyes remained riveted upon his. Several men who appeared to be ranch hands from the boss's property surrounded the four-poster bed upon which he and the woman were conjoined. Sitting atop a wooden fence railing that formed a perimeter around the bed, the rowdy men began cheering her on as though they were watching a rodeo as they ridiculed him in Spanish, Romanian, French, and a gibberish he did not recognize. He watched them exchanging currency while betting on his ability to satisfy the unearthly creature sucking out his manly fluids. When he finally convulsed and erupted into her demonically shaped mouth, she began hovering over him at a higher elevation. She reached out to the ranch hands and took all the money being exchanged and put it into her mouth in a seductive manner. She swallowed, nodded to the group of men, and began laughing at him as he lay naked and confused on the bed.

CHAPTER 15
Phantasm

Southeast of the Jaramillos' casita, a two-hour horseback ride into a hilly area filled with caverns and cliffs, Darik sat next to his friend Fierce Night Sky, a member of the Sinagua people, a mystic whose native name he could neither pronounce nor spell.

Sunset was approaching, at most two hours away, as their legs dangled over a steep ledge. Fierce Night Sky told him stories about the men in his tribe who came before him, all in search of themselves, nearly all of whom had sat in this same spot over the centuries while examining their own lives in relation to the canyon far below and the western horizon that the two of them were facing. He pointed out that the recessed, seat-like impressions in the red rock upon which they sat were in the shape of asses and legs. These hollows had been worn into the surface by the countless tribe members who had made this same journey, some once, some many times over the prior centuries.

"Never seen anything so beautiful," Darik said without turning toward his Sinaguan comrade. "I don't feel like I'm part of the real world anymore."

Fierce Night Sky handed Darik a hand-carved wooden pipe with a long stem. He nodded for his young friend to inhale the savory smoke while embers glowed in the shallow bowl. Darik complied and felt his entire body undergo a tickling sensation like the pins and needles he used to experience after remaining in one position too long while carving birdhouses.

"Shit," he said in a blissful tone, "I don't know what I'm supposed to feel, but that one shot from my toes to my forehead! It missed everything in between. I don't even feel like I'm here sitting with you. I feel like I'm flying. Feel like I'm flying over my grandfather's forest watching him walk through the tall trees in search of something. Maybe a tree. Maybe me. I can't tell."

Fierce Night Sky raised his eyebrows as he stared at Darik, but no words were spoken. He simply listened.

During their ride to the canyon, Darik had sipped several mouthfuls of a honey-like liquid from the dried, hand-painted gourd that hung over Fierce Night Sky's shoulder. They eventually tied their horses to a scrub oak and walked up the fractured and irregular rock pathway that led to the summit where they now sat.

"Was that some sort of sweet whiskey?" Darik asked as lightheadedness circulated above his shoulders, his body wobbled, and he began shaking. "Not sure if it's the stuff in the pipe or that drink, but I'm going to pass out! Don't let me fall! Please don't let me fall! I don't want to fall!"

Fierce Night Sky leaned toward him. "You must fall, brother," he whispered. "You must let go of everything, my brother, and trust that you'll find the deepest corner of the dark pit where you've hidden all your life. The pit you've never faced. You will not be hurt. You feel a deep sadness right now. But since you won't let go of the pain from your losses, there is no way for you to know who you really are. You have no understanding. Your truths remain hidden. This makes you lame. You are unable to move with grace within yourself or with your daughter. You have stopped listening to your other family, the trees. You no longer share your thoughts with them, and this keeps you entirely alone."

Darik felt himself being laid onto his back by at least a dozen hands, two of which he was certain must have belonged to Fierce Night Sky. He drifted into a lucid dream filled with unfamiliar, eerie harmonic tones, flashing lights and colors, and a dizzying array of human and animal figures. Although he could not hear any individual voice with clarity, he felt a vibration surging through his body that seemed to be musical, but he knew it was not music made by any instrument he had ever heard. A harmony of sounds resonated within his body in a way that encased him in this altered reality.

Through the hallucinations within this semi-lucid dream state, Darik saw a fire burning far below. A small house ablaze in a forest was emitting flames that reached high above the treetops. The individual rope-like threads forming the thatched roof of the house glowed in an array of bright colors as smoke filled the air.

A tall, bearded man and a much shorter, beautiful black-haired woman stood far from the flames. An infant wrapped in a small quilt was in her arms. Darik could not see the baby's facial features through the smoke. The couple did not look familiar and yet they did. He watched as they eventually turned, tears streaming down their faces, and slowly walked in the other direction while the burning structure was reduced to a pile of glowing embers. They made their way across a field to a structure Darik knew well, his grandparents' farmhouse outside Bucharest. The man and woman's faces began to display the familiar features of his grandparents in their forties, the age when Darik became their full responsibility. Darik could now see through the house's roof as though it was made of solid glass. He watched the woman place the baby into a hand-built wooden cradle with artistic figures etched into its outer surface. She rocked the cradle as the infant's soft whimpering shifted into the beautiful sounds of a baby entering sleep.

Darik's body clenched as an unrelenting pain settled in the lowest part of his abdomen as these images took over his thoughts. Within a few moments he turned to his side and began vomiting up a rancid, grayish-green fluid, thick as mud, that burned like fire as it oozed through his nostrils and mouth. His five senses became intertwined, and he thought he had lost control of his bladder, certain he had begun pissing wildly on himself. Yet, at the same time, it felt as though his bladder was not functioning. He sensed multiple hands massaging his body and felt as though he were a farm horse being rubbed down after an exhausting day of plowing. A relentless humming sound filled his head and caused the dizziness to increase as he lay coiled up like a rope hanging from the side of a saddle.

Tears welled in his eyes as he lay in a fetus-shaped position on the hard rocky surface, icy cold to the point of stinging. As he struggled to open his eyes, he realized that a profound blurriness was carrying him deeper into this terrifying stupor.

"Fall. Let go of everything," he heard his friend whisper. "You are still detached from your true feelings. You must reach into your fear, my brother, to be whole before you can feel anything. Take fear into your hands and bring it into your heart so you can finally know what prevents you from filling your emptiness with the love of the Great Spirit that will protect you if you allow it to occur."

His heart pounded like a drum. His body shook violently. Certain he was going to roll off the ledge and fall to his death, he cried out, "Who am I? Why did they die? Why have all of them died and left me alone?" He wailed as he imagined a dozen or more hands tapping his body, patting him into a calmer state of being. "Did I do something wrong to make this happen? To keep happening? Why am I alive? Why has everyone left me? They are dead and I survived. I'm so sorry. I would have given my life to protect them. I would have," he repeated through his tears.

"Not your journey. Theirs," his companion replied. "You were part of it just as they have been part of yours. But your destiny was never their destiny. My destiny was never the same as the two wives I have lost or of my mother and father who left the Earth when I, too, was a child, or the departure of all the others who've joined me on this journey."

Darik could hear Fierce Night Sky trying to assuage his fear as intense, jolting pain rushed through his body. The sensation of falling over the cliff became intensely real, and, as he tightened up, his shoulders and legs began cramping while he twisted and turned on the rocky surface.

Dry heaves racked his body as pent up fear was squeezed out during his hallucinations and relieved him of toxic memories and substances circulating through his arteries and veins. This continued for what seemed like many hours, although Fierce Night Sky would later tell Darik after he had returned from this dark journey, that the entire episode lasted only a few minutes in what the white settlers considered to be time. Fierce Night Sky had explained to Darik during a prior hike, one without the aid of hallucinogens, that he did not trust the white man's notion of time any more than he trusted the whites' concepts of life or of death.

Fierce Night Sky, his spiritual brother and the trusted guide accompanying him through this gauntlet of pain and sorrow that began when Darik began inhaling from the ornate pipe after sipping the liquid concoction of local mushrooms in the dried gourd, shared virtually nothing about the details of this ancient, time-tested ritual that produced unique experiences for every man in the Sinagua tribe who had taken this journey over the centuries. He later admitted that until this very day he had been unsure whether Darik was ready for this journey and that it was only after Darik expressed some degree of shame when he admitted he had been having sex with Mrs. Jaramillo ever since his arrival in Sedona, all the while knowing her husband was aware of it, that he determined Darik was ready.

"Darik, Mrs. Jaramillo uses the skill of a sorceress to keep you trapped in her soulless womb. She has been removing your life energy through sex, as well as your will to be truthful with yourself, both of you aware that her angry husband was lying in his bed in the casita listening to you fucking like wild animals."

Once Darik had shared the details about Mrs. Jaramillo earlier in the afternoon, Fierce Night Sky determined that in order for Darik to extricate himself from her evil forces, it was time for his young friend to explore the darkness that had enveloped him since he was an infant, a darkness from which he never grieved, never celebrated, and never fully embraced life.

"A giant bird, an eagle, a big one about the size of a pony, plucked me up from the cliff with his talons as I sat with you," Darik explained.

"It was a male? How did you know it was not a female, some sort of goddess or witch that lifted you from the cliff?"

Darik was puzzled. "I think of eagles as men, but I don't know why. Of course there have to be females to lay the eggs. I don't know, I just thought it was a male. Either way, the eagle carried me to a nest made of barbed wire on a mountaintop spitting glowing rocks and liquid from its guts…"

"…A volcano," Fierce Night Sky interrupted. "Much of my homeland and that of my ancestors is covered with volcanoes although none have awakened during my lifetime. I know of the spirits who live in these volcanoes—how they make themselves erupt when the human beings on this planet need to be reminded about their place in the whole order of everything."

"No volcanoes in Romania where I was born and raised. This is the first time I've seen one in real life or my dreams," Darik replied.

"No difference between what you call dreams and what you consider real life. I have never visited your homeland, but there are volcanoes whether you see them or not. Mother Earth is covered with these beauty marks and scars. They are similar to the grief you have denied and have kept hidden since you were a baby. These earth marks cover our powerful lands, above and below the ground. They cover the deserts and are attached to the bottoms of the big waters you call oceans, and they form many of the lakes. She, our Mother Earth, decides when it is time to teach us these important lessons. We are one people. All people. One race. No race. All humans walk the Earth with all living things, all the things the whites do not think are alive like the rocks, the sand, the soil, and, of course, the trees. The white man often loses sight of how he fits into things because of his ignorance, stubbornness, and fear.

"Fear is so powerful and dangerous. You live in fear, Darik. Always in fear. You hide from it and from your grieving. You do not think so because you have ventured a long distance from your homeland to mine to escape. You are strong. You like adventures. But you live in fear of the end of all things, of all time. You think being born is the beginning and that dying and being buried is the end. You have never embraced the idea that death of the body is not an ending but simply another beautiful part of life for all things."

"But in the dream I saw my parents die," Darik said tearfully. "I never knew how or why they vanished from my life. My grandparents were there and always there for me, but neither told me what happened."

"And what if they had told you the story of that home burning to the ground and your parents dying? What would you have done differently? Would you have not left your homeland at some point? Would you have not been struck by lightning? Would you not have met and loved Lihua, the woman who died in the fire? Would you have not married and made a child with your wife, Ingrid? Would you have not gotten on your horse and journeyed to this area to fuck the sorceress at the casita? Would you have not ridden with me and smoked from my pipe and drank from the painted gourd and begun to face your darkness?"

"I don't know," Darik answered. "I've never thought about it before. Too busy growing up on the farm helping my grandparents and learning about the forest and learning the language of the trees and the stories they shared. I never knew what it was to grieve, to mourn someone, to let go and feel deep sorrow as part of the healing. It's not something I knew anything about."

"That eagle you spoke of, I think it was female," said Fierce Night Sky. "I think you now know it was Mrs. Jaramillo disrupting your dreams and that she was sucking life out from your manhood in what you imagined to be pleasurable sex. She was luring your dark spirit into her volcano, nesting you in barbed wire from which you would never escape and find yourself.

"My young friend," Fierce Night Sky continued, "I met a white man long ago who told me stories from another land, who knows, maybe your homeland? He told me that long ago, as long ago as the ancient ones in my nation roamed these lands or maybe longer, that an evil goddess, a witch-like creature called a succubus, stole the hearts of men through seduction, even the strongest ones, one at a time, by offering the warm cave of her womanhood to them. Then she sucked life from each man as he mixed up his pleasure with the death of his essence. It was not until a man was able to awaken from this rape by the succubus that he realized the part of himself he gave up without a warrior's fight was not the sticky white source of life he put into that woman's womb but a part of his soul that would need to be replenished by living life with a more pure heart. But that is a journey that not all men are strong enough to even attempt nor complete successfully."

"She…Mrs. Jaramillo…she's a sorceress?"

"That is not for me to say. You have to look within yourself and decide what it was you gave to her and what she intended to steal from you that her husband could no longer give to her. Maybe never could or never did. Maybe she is a demon who seeks dominion over weak men. Maybe, yes, some sort of sorceress. But my friend, what you experienced in your dreams were painful thoughts created by never grieving, by never healing yourself, by continuing to hide from the pain of your losses. Instead of searching for and finding your whole self, something that has escaped your grasp for so long, you have chosen to dwell in a dangerous trap you set for yourself, a place where you remain hidden, willingly hidden, although you might not have realized it, with sad stories about your isolation. White people call it pity. I think of it of as a start to healing. But it can only happen if you are willing to look it in the eye, see what it represents, and set it free.

"Darik, my friend, that is the witch, your isolation. It is not Mrs. Jaramillo and it is not the eagle. You have tried many times to punish your own soul because of the sorrow you have kept hidden. I do not think you have ever felt real joy—even from your daughter. You have never allowed yourself to be honest about your feelings. None of it. Not the pain, sorrow, joy or love, not even the pleasure you experienced with Lihua or Ingrid, and not Mrs. Jaramillo. None of them. You live your life in the fog of fear as though you are awaiting the arrival of the next sadness, the next loss, or the next disappointment. You bring this upon yourself as a punishment. You cause it to occur over and over by believing this is your eternal path, and you have come to depend on it to keep you harnessed in fear. You let it happen. You seek it out. But you have choices. You made one coming here to this canyon and to this ledge on this day. Now you must decide where to go next on your journey to reclaim your humanness and to allow your soul to grow like the trees in the forests all over Mother Earth that tell you stories, that try to tell you the truth. It is time to listen to the trees and to your heart. Listen more carefully. That is the key; at least that is what I believe."

Darik stared, never uttering a word.

"Your soul….not your ears," Fierce Night Sky continued, "allows you to hear the voices of the trees and of life itself. But you've done this without learning anything, any of the truth for yourself because your heart remains closed. It is shut down. You have blocked the realities of your life from guiding or teaching you to actually live fully in each moment. That is what I think. But I do not know. It is your life and your fear, not mine. Only what you learn for yourself is what matters. No more questions to me. No more talk. Lay back and watch the spirits in the sky dance like stars."

"But those are stars. I wouldn't know what a spirit looks like."

Fierce Night Sky smiled. He raised and lowered his arms as though he was the eagle. He tilted his head back and shouted out the wild sounds of a bird of prey, an eerie song comprised of a few joyful notes and said, "Look around. You live among the spirits. Everywhere. Everything."

Hank Fisher

A herd of golden bison remained motionless atop a body of blue water adjacent to a large sandy beach. They stood securely as though the surface of the water was solid. They appeared to be statues and did not display the characteristics of living creatures. Oceanlike waves pounded a long, narrow beach covered with onyx-colored sand, leaving behind miles of thin white bubbling threads that moved like snakes over dry land. He was floating on a raft made of large tree trunks from the Romanian forest where he learned to carve birdhouses. He heard numerous voices coming from mouths that had formed on the upper surface of the raft. The voices were speaking at the same time in his native tongue, but the roaring sound of the waves made it impossible to decipher what they were actually saying. On top of three of the buffaloes, one per animal, sat three beautiful, naked women. Their perfectly shaped bodies reflected the shimmering ocean saltwater mist that saturated the air. They, too, were motionless. He could not tell if they were actual women or were carved mannequins.

CHAPTER 16
Odyssey

Darik estimated that the horseback ride from Sedona to Denver, a distance of six hundred miles, would take thirty days to complete, possibly a little more. As a result of what he experienced during his clifftop journey with Fierce Night Sky, he realized when he saddled up an hour before dawn that time was neither an ally nor an adversary. His early departure allowed him to avoid having to explain his sudden decision to leave to Mrs. Jaramillo.

He rode from sunrise to sunset some days while on others he would dismount, set up camp, and immerse himself for hours carving new birdhouses out of wood he gathered during the long ride. He slept under the stars wherever possible but also stayed overnight in several small encampments along the trails in northern Arizona and southern Colorado that were typically comprised of small mud thatch huts large enough for one person, two at most, and a few supplies.

Throughout the ride, he revisited his inexplicable journey on the cliff with Fierce Night Sky, continuing to seek meaning he could attach to his experiences in Sedona, including Mrs. Jaramillo. He avoided the heavily traveled trails on the trip back toward Denver, instead choosing to follow thin, narrow side trails etched through the underbrush and back country by coyotes, bear, deer and antelope, often detouring from his intended path so he could ride through large, forested areas overflowing with statuesque pines, cottonwoods, and colorful aspens that blanketed the hillsides as he entered Colorado through its southwestern border. He used the long horseback ride to confront his thoughts and to sort out the implication of the hallucinations Fierce Night Sky had led him through, as well as making determinations about what he wanted for his life with his daughter, Theresa, whom he had not seen in months.

His intention was to return to Eagle Trail Ranch, even if only briefly, and explain to Mulroony and Silvano why he fled the ranch five years earlier to mourn Lihua. He anticipated then riding to the area adjacent to Mrs. Brown's property southwest of Denver to climb the cottonwood tree he assumed would have more than doubled in height during the nearly five years since he last saw it, and leave a love note in the birdhouse with his name and Lihua's etched into its roof.

Darik reached Pueblo, one of the largest cities in Colorado, on the twenty-fifth day of his ride, placing him one hundred miles due south of Eagle Trail Ranch, a four or five-day ride that he hoped would be void of the severe dry heat he had experienced during his meandering ride through the high desert plains.

He found a boarding house in midtown Pueblo and enjoyed a steak and potatoes dinner at a nearby cafe before turning in that first night.

Sleep, even on an actual bed for the first time in nearly a month, did not come easily. After tossing and turning for several hours, well past midnight, he sat up, lit a kerosene lamp, withdrew his carving tools from the satchel within his saddlebag, and continued working on one of six small birdhouses, each measuring no more than nine inches deep by six inches wide by eight or nine inches in height, that he had begun carving after he left Sedona, the first carvings he had attempted in the years since Lihua's death.

The interior of the birdhouse was completed by dawn. His next task was to refine the exterior surface so he could then begin final detailing as soon as possible, ideally before reaching Denver. Two of the birdhouses were made from aspen, two from piñon pine, and two from cottonwood, of which one was nearly finished. Each birdhouse possessed the distinctive artistry for which he had gained recognition in his Romanian village as a child and again later while working at the Eagle Trail Ranch.

His urge to carve had remained dormant for five years, but his drug induced excursion with Fierce Night Sky had revived his desire to reconnect with wood carving, an essential element of his internal journey that was reawakened during his travel between Sedona and Denver that would eventually take him back to Tejada. His plan was to sell each of the completed birdhouses either to small shops or individuals he might come in contact with during the long ride.

He had saved forty-eight dollars doing odd jobs such as repairing fences, barns, and roofs while in route to Sedona, and once there saved another eighty-five dollars working for the Jaramillos and other locals.

He had not anticipated entering into an adulterous relationship in Sedona with his employer's wife, but he now realized that what she extracted from him was not worth the free room and board plus the fifteen dollars a week he was paid. Yet he also recognized that she was the first woman with whom he had sex since Ingrid's illness began. Even though he repeatedly weighed the benefits of being intimate with Mrs. Jaramillo, it was not until his experience on the Sedona clifftop that he finally began to understand and, to a degree, appreciate his grief.

* * *

"What's that you were doing all night?" the owner of the boarding house asked when Darik came downstairs the next morning with the bulging saddle bag over his shoulder. "Not like you were loud, but I heard rustling around through my bedroom ceiling. I'm a bit curious."

Darik looked at the older woman whose face displayed the wear and tear of living in an arid climate. "Just carving a bit. Didn't mean to disturb you. Couldn't sleep. Figured I'd occupy my time usefully."

"Carving what?"

He opened the saddle bag and withdrew the nearly completed cottonwood birdhouse that was his companion during the restless night.

"Lordy, lordy, lordy, boy. That's as good as I've ever seen. I've seen whittling but nothing like this. How'd you ever learn to make one of these without a hammer and nails?"

"My grandfather taught me. Been carving since I was a kid. This is the first I've done in a few years. Still a bit rusty. Next ones will be better."

"That I gotta see. Can't imagine anything better than this. How much you charge? I want one for the finches perched on the roofline over there. You can see them through the window. They've been here for months. I don't feed 'em. They just like it here. A birdhouse would be a nice addition to the place. How much?"

Having not yet considered a selling price and somewhat unwilling to part with one at this stage of his ride to Denver, he picked what he thought was a number too high for the woman.

"Seven dollars each. It's expensive, but they take me a long time. First I have to find the right limb or hunk of wood to cut a block. Then I have to rough it out and shape it. And then what takes the most time is carving out the inside so it's as perfect as I can make it. Don't tell nobody, but the outside is the easiest part. That's where the art is. The interior is functional because I don't want any splinters to hurt the birds. I know the price is…."

"Hush. Hush. Seven dollars ain't cheap, but that's one of a kind. I could get ten dollars for it at the general store. If I had a bunch of 'em, I'd make a good profit. My husband and I own the general store. He runs it and stays out of my way here. He's a nuisance and is better off fiddling around over there. He's always looking for something new to sell, usually something from around these parts, usually something an Indian or some Mexican made. Something like your birdhouse can't be gotten from Denver or Kansas City. And even if we order something through a catalog, it takes months to ship here whether it's by train or coach. How many you got? How much for the whole bunch?"

"I'm flattered and don't want you to get me wrong, but I'm not ready to sell any just yet. Still working on this one and have a bit of work left on the others in the saddle bag. I want to sell a couple on the way to Denver and then maybe sell the rest of them once I'm there. I used to live near Denver. Lots of small shops and wealthy people there. I'm guessing I'd be able to get a bit more, maybe eight-fifty there. If shopkeepers can sell them for fifteen to some high society family, they'll be happy."

"Sonny, we're all in business to make money, same as the shopkeepers in Denver. Don't need some young cowboy explaining commerce to me. No offense. Give me a price I can live with, and I'll give you back your money from last night's stay and pay you in cash right now for that birdhouse once you finish it up. But I'd like 'em all."

"There's still a few days of work left for the others, and I want to get back on the trail."

"Free room and board until you finish them up. How's that for an offer? Hell, your room costs a dollar a night and that includes breakfast and a bath. I'll give you three days and nights, more if you need them, if you'll sell me all six at a fair price. That'll lighten your saddle bags for the ride, and you'll have some money in your pocket. You can find more wood on the ride north and start carving new ones. How much?"

"Really. I don't want to sell them all just yet."

"Fine. Keep one and finish up five for me. I'll pay seven dollars each. That'd be thirty-five dollars. Maybe I can get twelve dollars each. That's a nice profit for us without doing any extra work. Lots easier on this old body to sell birdhouses than to cook and clean all day. And unless you're some fool and spend your money on drinking and whoring between here and Denver, you'll be able to take your time to find a decent place to live there. Who knows, maybe get on with another shopkeeper who wants to be the only person selling these carvings. Come on, cowboy, don't bullshit me. Deal or no deal? Hell, I'll even wash those smelly clothes. They smell like horse crap. You go up to that same room, carve your young heart away, and I'll wash up everything you got."

Darik had already realized his clothes smelled like he'd been on the trail for a month. "Where's your husband's store?" he asked. "I need new clothes, especially if you're going to take all these for washing."

"Child, don't be bashful. Raised six sons. Carve buck naked up there for all I care. Nothing you got that I ain't seen a thousand times before."

He smiled, blushed a bit, and replied, "I might just do that. But I still need to get some new clothes. Not sure how long I'll be in Denver before I head back down to Tejada. It's just across the New Mexico border. That's where my daughter lives. She's staying with a friend while I'm out here."

"Fine," she replied. They shook hands on the deal, "Gurney's the name. Short for Gurneath. Yours?"

"Darik. Came to Colorado nearly fifteen years ago. I'm from Romania."

"Ain't no difference where you're from. Seem like a good young man. You got a daughter and are heading back to her. I like that. What about your wife?"

"Dead. Consumption. Only twenty."

"Life's not fair. That's how it is out here. How come you ain't found another wife, someone to mother your daughter? You whoring around?"

He hesitated. "No. I met a woman in Arizona but it wasn't a good situation."

"Married? Some unhappy bitch doing it with you instead of her husband. Right? You're a handsome cowboy, I suppose. When I was younger, way younger, I might've snuck off with you too. Her husband figure it out and want to shoot you? That why you left wherever you were?"

"Sedona. No," he chuckled. "It was just time to head home. I'm just not interested in being with someone like her. Never really liked whoring around neither as I got older. When I was young and not in love with anyone special, things were different. Ever hear of Louviers?"

"Sure. It's on the rail line to Denver. Big cattle ranches. That where you worked?"

"Not far from there. A few miles this side of Littleton."

"Don't mean to be nosy but, shit, I'm that way by nature. I know a young woman here in Pueblo. She's a bit younger than you. Spirited as a wild horse but in a good way. Doesn't follow any rules. Don't get me wrong, she's a good girl with a heart of gold. She seems to live to break rules. More like a man in that way than a young filly. Her daddy owns a big spread a little west of here on the way to Florence. Beautiful place. She's got four older brothers, too, each of them married and with sons. She's a young widow and don't like any of the men around here. Not at all. Her brothers guard her like she's a child and her daddy's worse, but they're all true gentlemen. Scottish. Different than most the men around here. But she can't breathe without them trying to tell her how to inhale. They forget she was married at sixteen to a nice young buck. He died the night of their wedding. He was a few years older than her, probably your age. She sunk pretty deep for a couple years, and now that she's got her legs back under her, she's reclaiming herself if that makes any sense. Strong young woman. Most men don't have the smarts or patience to handle her, and she doesn't suffer for fools if you know what I mean. Most of 'em just want her for breeding and nothing else. Not sure you'd like her or that she'd find you halfway appealing, and I don't have a clue about your taste in women. Tell you the truth, she's got an eye for beautiful things; that's something she's got. Her family's house is full of beautiful art, and she's the one who's been responsible for finding it. But nothing that resembles your birdhouses."

"Nice of you to say so. Appreciate it. But I'm not interested in meeting her. I've got to take care of personal matters when I get to Denver. I don't want to be fooling around with anyone. I need to keep things simple."

"I'm not a marriage broker, boy, and nothing about life's simple. That's just plain damn silly. I'm just trying to say that knowing Vida the way I do, I'll bet she'll buy at least one of those birdhouses from me, maybe more. So hush up. Whether you like it or not, I'm gonna let her know about these carvings when she's in town in two or three days. Comes in with the buckboard to stock up her pantry."

Darik shrugged. "You can show her the first birdhouse once it's finished, and when I'm done with the others you can sell them all to her if you'd like, but I don't want to meet her. Like I said, I'm trying to tie up loose ends in Denver and don't need distractions."

"Cowboy, she might not even like you. In fact, with that attitude, I'll have to give it more thought. Hell, you might seem like tumbleweed to her. Don't get up in arms."

"I'm not meaning to be rude. I'm just not interested. Maybe down the road, maybe not."

She laughed. "For a smart young cowboy or one who thinks he is, you don't know shit. Time's passing you by even if you've been grieving your late wife. It's a lot like the Arkansas River that's close by—ebbs, flows, dries up, and floods the lowlands some years. But it's not predictable. One thing's for damn sure, none of us get a lot of chances to float downstream or cross to the other side of this river of life. You better figure it out. Time ain't real and sure ain't what it appears to be. Deceptive as the horizon during a dust storm or a winter blizzard. Sometimes it looks endless and peaceful, sometimes not. But this old lady learned long ago that the timing for most things ain't what we hope for. Hell, look at us. You were checking out a couple minutes ago, about to pay me for the room, and now you're going to stay for a few days, carve up some birdhouses for me, and then hit the trail. Did you plan any of this? I don't think so. Timing's everything. None of us can control it, so we shouldn't bullshit ourselves about it."

"Am I supposed to answer you?" he asked rhetorically.

"Nope," she grinned knowingly, "just consider my sermon part of the free room and board, kind of like going to school though I don't know if you're the slightest bit educated. So don't be talking back. Now, drag your sorry ass on over to my husband's store and get some new clothes. Tell him I sent you and to give you his best price. When you get back, give me the ones you're wearing so I can wash the stink out of them if that's even possible."

Hank Fisher

Young women, elegantly dressed in formal gowns and wearing beautifully jeweled necklaces and matching hair combs, were waltzing with calvary officers clad in their finest uniforms. Music similar to what was played in Bucharest at the summer festivals during his youth filled the ballroom. He was attired in worn-out denims covered by chaps, a leather vest, and oxhide boots and was standing alone in a far corner of the large ballroom. He felt invisible to the people enjoying the formal affair. To his surprise, one of the walls was suddenly transformed into two hinged swinging bar doors, huge ones, each the size of a barn door. The head of a beautiful golden palomino pushed through as the doors opened. The horse scanned the entire room as though it was looking for someone. The music stopped as the beautiful animal made its way into the ballroom. It bowed down as if curtsying. The elegant young women and their dancing partners turned toward it for a moment and then resumed dancing as the music began again. The horse backed out through the swinging doors until it was no longer visible. The doors dissolved back into the wall as though they had never existed.

CHAPTER 17
Serendipity

Two of the remaining five birdhouses were completed by the afternoon of the third day, Thursday. Each time Darik presented Gurneath with a finished birdhouse she behaved as though she was attending a livestock auction, examining each birdhouse from top to bottom and side to side. She reached into her pocket each time and handed him the money she owed.

Darik spent seven dollars at the general store for new clothes, a new shirt, britches, bandana, and a leather vest. In order to break in the pants, he decided to stroll the streets surrounding the store. He walked past the boarding house where Gurneath was standing at the entrance with her husband, both waving for him to come over. He nodded but continued heading the other direction.

Although he did not holster a pistol, Darik always rode with his Winchester strapped in the scabbard. He also carried a hunting knife with a beautifully etched nine-inch blade attached to a hand-carved elk antler handle that he bought in Castle Rock just before he married Ingrid. With extra money in his pocket, he was contemplating purchasing a new knife even though he had no real need for it. He felt like he should have something new to earmark his decision to finally let go of the memories of Lihua and Ingrid and finally coming to terms with what had occurred years earlier to his own parents.

Darik had visited the Pueblo gunsmith shop the day he arrived, and in addition to a fine selection of firearms, he was pleased at the quality of knives in the display case. He re-entered the shop, tipped his hat to the proprietor, a grizzled looking man with a corn cob pipe dangling from his lips, and asked if he could look at the knives a little more closely.

"That's why they're here. Look at 'em. Don't cut yourself. I ain't a doctor."

"Me neither. I'm a wood carver. Pretty handy with sharp tools, knives included."

"You're the one Gurneath's been bragging about. Made you into some sort of legend. I want to see one of those birdhouses. Might be willing to trade you a knife for one if they're as good as she claims. Want to deal?"

"They're up in my room. Still have to finish a couple for her. Tell you what, I'll come back when I'm done and you can look take a look. Then maybe we can deal. She's selling them at the general store for twelve dollars."

"Seems high. But she's smart enough to always make a profit. You and me…we'll make our own deal. Fair enough?"

"Sure. Mind if I look around?"

"Just remember, go outside to bleed. Don't want blood wrecking my floor. Bad for business."

Darik looked through the inventory and narrowed his choice to two knives—one with a narrow seven-inch long straight blade with spectacular scrimshaw etched into its ivory handle; the other, slightly shorter, featured a more distinctive curved shape and was adorned with elaborate designs etched into the metal that resembled calligraphy.

"Kind of ladylike, that second one," a woman's voice commented sarcastically, "especially for a rugged looking cowboy like you, a wood carver, I'm told. A man of nature, I suppose. Kind of surprised you're not looking for a long-bladed Bowie knife to fend off birdhouse thieves."

He turned and looked up into the face of a young redheaded woman. "Miss, with all due respect to your beautiful eyes, I'm surprised nobody ever told you that the size of a man's blade has nothing to do with his ability to use it. I say that as politely as possible since you're a lady."

"Gurneath was right. You're the real polite type. Measure up nicely by cowboy standards. Some of the most courteous men I've ever known, including my father and brothers, are cowboys through and through. Never heard a one of them cuss in my presence. Now what they might say at a bar or on horseback, that's anyone's guess."

"Very kind of you, Miss. Thanks. How'd you happen to be talking about me with Gurneath? You kin?"

"Nope. I'm Vida, the gal you don't want to meet. She's curious why you're pretending not to want to meet a paying customer, at least a possible one. Thinks you're kind of bashful. But I don't… the bashful part. Kinda good looking but maybe not the pick of the litter. Yep. But shy? Not at all…."

"….I once knew an old woman," he interrupted, "in the village near my grandfather's farm in Romania who could see the future and describe the past. She had a certain way of separating the truth from lies and exaggerations."

She smiled. "You think I'm not telling you the truth, Cowboy? I don't have a crystal ball or magic potions. I rely on a little observation with common sense. Plenty of both in fact. And eyes don't lie. Not a bit. I can plainly see that your eyes are sharp enough to cut through a woman's heart as easily as your carving tools cut through wood."

Realizing that he might sound arrogant, he replied, "I apologize, Miss. It wasn't that I didn't want to meet you; I wasn't trying to meet anyone just now. Just trying to get a few things done, make a little money, and ride up to Denver."

"Gurneath wasn't making a marriage proposal on my behalf, Cowboy. Just thought I might like the birdhouses. And I do. Beautiful work. Never seen anything quite like them. She also thought you could use a friend while you're in Pueblo, at least for a hot meal or something like that."

"Like that?"

"Like that."

"She doesn't know me well at all but probably told you that I'm stubborn," Darik said. "Would take more than those green eyes of yours to make me change plans."

She batted her eyelids flirtatiously a couple times. "Was hoping you weren't too easy. Good to know you're a man of principle and seem to be good with a compliment from a stranger too."

He nodded and said, "Darik."

"I'm Vida. It means *dearly loved* in Scottish. I was born in Scotland. Pleased to meet you, Darik. We're both foreigners. How about that? I was two when my father brought the entire family over from Scotland. He came to Colorado so he could buy a large spread to raise cattle and horses. He's quite good at it."

"I know a little about Scotland," he replied. "Never met anyone from there. How do you like it here?"

She smiled. "Nothing to compare it to. I was an infant when we came to Pueblo. This place is downright boring. At least the mountains aren't far away and the Arkansas River's a godsend. I was in Denver one time. Big place. Lots to do. A cowboy like you could get in some real trouble there. Family in Denver? That why you're heading there?

Darik was surprised how comfortable he felt speaking on such a personal basis with this young woman of maybe nineteen or twenty. "Loose ends. I got a few things to take care of there and at the ranch where I used to work. It's south of Denver in a hilly area between Louviers and Littleton. Eagle Trail Ranch."

"Do you mind?" she asked as she slid her arm into his and led him away from the display case of knives. He did not resist. "How long you been on the trail?"

"Too many months," he answered. "Moved to Tejada a few years back. It's a small village in northern New Mexico right along the Rio Concho about a hundred miles south of here. Nothing to do there. Hell, Pueblo's wild compared to Tejada. It's not far from the Kit Carson Trail. I haven't been back to Denver in five years. Think I'll be there for a few days. Not really sure. No schedule. Want to check on something and sell a few birdhouses. Then I'll head back to Tejada. Got a daughter there. She's almost five. Haven't seen her in months. I miss the hell out of her."

"Daughter? Never figured you for the marrying type."

"Didn't know I was until it happened at a time when settling down just seemed right. But I lost my wife a while back. I felt lost after that and needed to get my head on straight so I could be the kind of father that my daughter needs. Theresa's as beautiful as the springtime and smart as could be. A friend's taking care of her while I'm gone. Don't know if this makes sense to a woman because women are so much better at being parents then men are—at least I think so—but I needed to sort things out after burying my wife. But I'm sure you don't want to hear about that."

"Why wouldn't I? Not like I can't carry on a conversation."

"I didn't mean that. Just didn't think a woman would want to hear some sad story about another woman. Things like that."

"It's not like you ran out on her or there's wanted posters out for you for being a bad husband or father. Let's talk. I'll bet you haven't spoken about your wife with anyone at all. Have you?"

He shook his head. "Not really. Only once in Sedona. And it wasn't a normal conversation. Was with an Indian wise man, a friend. We were sitting on a ledge above the Red Rock Canyon. Beautiful place, maybe the most magical I've ever been to. I sipped some sort of cactus drink he mixed up, and then we smoked something, but it wasn't tobacco. The stuff made me a bit loco. I had no idea that would happen. Did me in for a few hours. Don't remember the details of our conversation, not exactly, but the dreams in it woke me up to my life in a bunch of ways."

She tilted her head with a confused look.

"Vida, would you like some coffee? I don't drink beer or whiskey these days, at least not much of either. Something about you makes me feel safe if that makes sense. That's not usually the case with strangers."

"I've got time right now," she replied. "I'd like to find out more about your daughter and the birdhouses. If this isn't an imposition, maybe I can get you to carve up a special one for my father before you head out. His birthday is next week."

"We'll work something out."

With their arms linked, she led Darik to the entrance of a small cafe on the far side of the street. They sat at a corner table chatting about their marriages and their spousal losses. Their eyes were fixated on one another like long lost friends. Without any apprehension they revealed details of their lives until finally deciding to head back to the general store where her buckboard had been loaded by Gurneath's husband.

Darik looked directly into her eyes. "Pretty forward of me to ask, Vida, but do you have any plans for tomorrow?"

"Busy at the ranch tomorrow, but the day after, Saturday, is wide open. How about a picnic? There's a beautiful plateau overlooking the Arkansas River that's only a couple miles away from here."

She pulled out a sheet of stationery from the canvas bag attached to the seat in the buckboard and sketched a map.

"These directions make sense? I'm not good at drawing maps."

"It's fine. Looks like maybe a twenty-minute ride from the boarding house. That about right?"

"You got it, Cowboy. Glad you're not as unswayable as you led Gurneath to believe."

Vida was tall, only three inches shorter in her riding boots than Darik. Her red hair hung loosely below her shoulders. They shook hands and she leaned forward and gave him a friendly kiss on the cheek.

"What did I do to deserve that?" he asked.

"Not a thing. You didn't do a thing. Mostly you didn't say anything dumb like men often say to me, the ones who think they have a chance with me if you don't mind me saying so. All in all, you've done well for yourself."

Darik raised his eyebrows, bowed slightly, and told her that he'd meet her Saturday at the plateau at noon hour. "By the way, do I have a chance?"

She smiled and turned toward the other direction. "Probably not."

Darik watched in silence as she stepped up into the buckboard and guided the two horses out the other end of town.

He returned to the boarding house. Gurneath was standing at the front door as though she were waiting for him. "Didn't know you could smile. Must have been a good day. How's the carving going?"

"Great. Should have the fifth birdhouse done by morning. But I gotta get started on another one. Got another order."

"That so? Not selling to the competition are you?"

"Naw. Not yet. Special order. Couldn't disappoint this woman by saying no."

"She's not like any woman you've ever met, Darik. You're a straight talker and she's not much on bullshit. She's a lot like you."

"You do this for a living? Match folks up?"

The large kiln was made of flagstone slabs, small pieces fit together so precisely that it looked like a single piece of rock. It gave off an earthy fragrance as smoke poured from the top of its narrow chimney. Through the large opening in the front of the kiln, he could see dozens of colorful ceramic tiles being fired, their glazed surfaces shimmering. A one-legged man, tall, over six feet, dressed in ceremonial garb similar to what was worn by the shaman at the Tejada Pueblo who tried to use his magic to help Ingrid through her illness, was kneeling next to the kiln in front of an altar. He was chanting unfamiliar words in an eerily beautiful melody similar to the sound of coyotes seeking a mate. A meal was being served at a huge wooden tabletop resting upon ornate wrought iron legs. Dozens of people, all strangers, sat at the table with beer mugs in hand, looking back into his eyes. Three women, Lihua, Ingrid, and Vida, were dancing together arm in arm in a circle with a small child, Theresa, sitting in the center. Bright orange and red clouds crisscrossed an evening sky illuminated by the full moon. Turning back toward the kiln, he watched as another person, a woman who looked like the crone from his Romanian village, reached into the glowing embers bare-handed and pulled out the tiles, one at a time, without burning herself. She laid the tiles down on the ground, forming a beautiful abstract pattern, each tile fitting perfectly with the adjacent pieces.

CHAPTER 18
Consciousness

"Gurneath," Darik said as noon approached and he handed the older woman a birdhouse as he entered the kitchen, "here's the last one. Maybe my favorite though I don't know why. It's got more life in it than the others. Hope you like it."

She reached into her apron pocket and handed him several coins, the final payment for her birdhouses. "Maybe you'll ship me a few once you're back in Tejada? I'll buy as many as you can make. I'll even advance you some money right now. I trust you."

"If I carve enough of these, I'll figure out how to ship some to you. Don't mean to rush, but I've got to get cleaned up after I finish a detail or two on the new birdhouse. It's for…"

"I know who it's for, cowboy. The look on your face don't hide much. Poker's not your game, is it? Extend my best to Vida. When you heading to Denver? You can bunk here 'til Monday if you'd like. No other guests but you right now. Quiet as a funeral parlor around here, so I'm gonna shutter the place for the weekend. My husband and I are heading to my sister's ranch the next two days. Fend for yourself tonight and tomorrow. I'm puttin' up the closed sign. Here's a key to the front door. Hold on to it and your room key. I'll get 'em when I get back. Like I said, I'm gonna be at my sister's spread northeast of town overnight; maybe Sunday too."

Darik grabbed Gurneath by the shoulders, pulled her against his chest, and kissed her forehead. "You've treated me like an old friend since I got here. You even managed to fix me up with Vida for a picnic. Don't know how to thank you. I needed someone to kick my butt to get me out of my own way. Thanks."

She placed her hands on his cheeks, "Boy, maybe you're figuring this out. Maybe you're figuring out how to live again. This life is more than just taking one breath after another. Just know that you've always got a place here."

Darik returned to his room and worked for several hours. His hands danced in rapid, syncopated movements with the sharp carving tools. Since the birdhouse was intended for Vida's father, he created a more rugged looking exterior surface with tiny animal heads carved into the surface of each of the four walls: a wolf, a falcon, a bear, and a puma. It was after midnight when he applied a thin layer of the special oil he used to coat the birdhouses, knowing that it would need at least four hours to dry. He darkened the kerosene lamp and drifted into a deep sleep that lasted until an hour past sunrise, far later than he usually slept.

The boarding house was silent when he awakened, and as he expected neither Gurneath nor her husband were to be found. He went into the kitchen, fixed some coffee, ate a muffin, and returned to his room to get ready to meet up with Vida.

He wrapped the birdhouse in a piece of white muslin he purchased from Gurneath's husband, placed it in the saddlebag, and mounted his horse. Within twenty minutes he approached a small rise that led to a meadow adjacent to a white water section of the Arkansas River. In the distance he saw a large quilt, at least eight feet square, laid out on a patch of buffalo grass a few yards from a buckboard and swayback horse that he assumed were Vida's. A hand-written note was attached to the seat:

You'll find me just beyond the small grove of cottonwoods on the far side of the buckboard. Tie up your horse and come on over. V

The variable sounds of the river became less audible as he walked through a small clearing and into the meadow in search of Vida, his saddlebag hanging over his shoulder. He walked with the heightened anticipation of a child preparing to open a birthday gift. Though not giddy, he felt carefree. As he strolled through the knee-high grass, Darik was surprised that the beautiful meadow, overflowing with an array of wildflowers, enveloped him as he moved down a slight incline toward the edge of the small pond. He heard splashing and the sound of a woman's voice, "I'm over here, Darik," she called out. "Hope you're not shy."

He looked to his left just beyond some head-high bushes along the shore and saw what appeared to be a goddess waving to him, her head just above the water line.

"What are you doing in there?" he asked. "Thought you said we were going to picnic. You didn't say anything about swimming."

"I got here a while ago and thought this would be a great way to greet you. I love surprises."

"Let me think about this," he replied sarcastically.

"No time to ponder things. Time to get in the pond with me. Nice temperature and not too deep. Not muddy on the bottom."

He stood awestruck as Vida, a woman he perceived to be somewhat shy, moved slowly toward shore, one unhurried step after another, her head staying just above the water line.

Although he was mesmerized by Vida, he was drawn to a distant image of Lihua in the field when they made love in what seemed like a lifetime ago. He tried to erase her image, and though his eyes were focused on Vida, he felt conflicted because the vision of Lihua was so powerfully real.

Vida's face shimmered as water droplets ran down her cheeks, her eyes twinkling like miniature beacons as she looked directly into the sun and rose from the water still clothed in a white blouse and riding pants.

She laughed boisterously as she watched his expression change. "You look shocked. Must have thought I'd been skinny dipping. Typical man. Heck, I barely know you. You look as though you figured I was coming out of the water like a Greek goddess in all her naked glory."

He laughed. "Wasn't at all sure what I was going to see. I was trying to be a gentleman."

"Just don't get any ideas. I was just funnin' you."

The contrast between her relatively broad shoulders, tiny waistline, and full hips reminded him of a marble sculpture he had seen in a Bucharest museum as a young boy. Nothing about Vida seemed real.

"Just so you know, I've never done this for anyone. Not anyone."

"Which part?" he asked. "The rising from the water or meeting me for a picnic?"

She raised her eyebrows seductively in an alternating pattern. "I can't explain it, Darik, but something tells me that we're supposed to be together today. Right now. And whatever happens will happen and we aren't supposed to question it," she said in a whispered tone that captured his attention even more.

Without offering a reply, Darik reached down to the large blanket and threw it to her. "My smaller blanket's on the horse, so go ahead and use this to dry off."

She grabbed the blanket in mid-air, began patting herself dry, and then threw it back to Darik as she walked forward, moving within a couple inches of him.

She leaned forward and pressed her lips softly against his, and their arms wrapped so tightly about one another that they became a single body standing on the shore of the small pond.

"My goodness," she whispered into his ear. "I'm a virgin as you might have guessed and that ain't changing today. But feeling your lips like this is enough to make me realize how much I hate being alone. I'll be thrown out of the congregation if the pastor finds out we're up here together alone, especially me standing here soaked to the bone, but that'll only be after my father and brothers banish me from Pueblo, and that's only after they string you up," she said with a lusty laugh.

Darik stepped back and smiled. "Vida, you're beautiful. You remind me of springtime in the high country." As he spoke, his hands slid down her back just below her waistline before she cleared her throat to get his attention.

"Cowboy, I like being touched. I admit it. But both of us need to slow down. We barely know each other although it seems like we're companions. But we gotta slow down. You're heading out of Pueblo in a day or two, and I don't plan on getting my heart broken," she said in a gentle yet confident tone.

He acknowledged her comment with a knowing glance. "I don't disagree. I'm a bit torn because everything about me wants you, and I'm being honest, but neither of us needs anything more than a great kiss right now. And that was a great kiss!"

Darik's hands explored her face as she stroked his.

Darik teased her by placing his index finger on the end of her nose. "Last thing I want is for your father, your brothers, your pastor, and the city fathers to string me up for getting too friendly with you."

"Kind of funny," she said. "Here we are all alone and nobody else would ever know what might have happened. Coulda happened. Maybe that's what growing up's all about? I'm not sure. But mostly I want you for a friend. We can skip what might have been in our story for now. If the fates intervene down the road and you come back here after sorting out your life, then maybe we'll figure out what to do next."

He walked her to the buckboard, turned, and headed back in the other direction, saying, "Glad you brought dry clothes. Get changed and let me know when I can turn around. I'm starved and ready for lunch."

Darik had experienced raw, uninhibited sex at the brothel in Louviers, but it always seemed that the women displayed a contrived, mechanical approach to having sex with him compared to Vida's grace, charm, and ladylike style. He felt an intense sensation of lust shoot through him as he imagined what it would have been like to be Vida's lover.

"You been around a lot. I can tell," she said. "Probably sounds childish, but I had no idea, really none at all, about how powerful a kiss like that could be. No idea. All that hogwash the pastor says about unmarried women and men being together, I'm beginning to think he's wrong. This could be heaven, Darik. We'll have to see what happens down the road. That okay with you?"

Darik was sweating profusely, his eyes stinging from the salty drops that had begun rolling down his forehead. "Vida, I won't lie. I ain't meaning to sound like I'm bragging, but this is different, being here with you. And all we did was kiss."

"Guess it's what a musician would call a prelude. But that's as far as this is going today. Not sure I'd know what to do next," she said as she leaned her mouth next to his ear and gave him a small kiss. "Let's eat. Fried chicken, potato salad, watermelon, and a few biscuits. A feast fit for a king and queen."

He smiled. "No mistakes today. This is perfect. Whoever you finally pick for your partner will be one hell of a lucky fella. Last thing I'd ever want to do is hurt you, so yes, lunch is the best idea right now."

Darik was drawn to her tender nature, yet she expressed no embarrassment about being so candid with him. Her openness was novel compared to most women he had known, but it was clear that physical intimacy was not the path she wanted to pursue with him, at least not yet. Nonetheless, he relished the idea that for the first time in ages he was spending time with someone who possessed the essential qualities of womanhood he admired most: a perfect blend of toughness, intelligence, and beauty.

He was silent as Vida piled food onto a plate she placed on the blanket without taking her eyes off of his. Despite the seductive glances, memories of Lihua flashed through his mind. He turned away from Vida momentarily and closed his eyes. Although these physical sensations for Vida were intense, he could not escape the image of Lihua in his mind's eye, rather than being preoccupied with the stunning young woman sitting a few feet away. Through squinted eyes he glanced at Vida as she filled her own plate, trying as best he could to concentrate on her smile.

Despite his attempts to escape the recurring memories of Lihua and secondarily of Ingrid, his late wife, something about Vida triggered sensations that shifted wildly between an immediate sense of joy and the burden of sorrow he kept shielded from himself.

"My father loved my mother in ways that were so romantic. At least that's how my brothers described the way my parents were with one another," Vida said calmly while interrupting the daydreams where she could see he had drifted. "She died when I was two, just after we moved to America, so I only have their stories about her. Father told me that all marriages were pre-arranged in his village in Scotland. Everyone thought my parents were virgins, including their parents, and that they'd never been with anyone. But they had. With each other. A lot. They'd made an everlasting promise when they were fifteen without telling anyone else, a promise that they would spend their entire lives together as husband and wife no matter what the Church or their parents said."

"I think that's how my own grandparents lived their lives too," he said in a melancholy tone. "I don't even know if they're alive at this point. So much time has passed."

She placed her hand on his shoulder in a loving gesture. "My father has always tried to be honest with me, sometimes pretty raw and bare bones, and this was the case both before and after my husband died the day of my wedding. Did I tell you that I was just sixteen when it happened?

My father began assuring me after my husband's funeral that someday I'd find another man who'd steal my heart if I were open to it, kind of like you're doing right now. He knew that my late husband was the love of my life, but death has a way of shifting what we believe to be true, and what we learn is just part of the journey of getting older and wiser. But, of course, I'm only nineteen."

He sat silently and placed his hand on her shoulder. They smiled but said nothing.

"My father has told me repeatedly that I'd meet another man who might become my great love and that I'd then make choices about my life and that he wouldn't interfere or pass judgment as long as he felt I was safe and trusted whomever I was with. I don't think he figured I'd come this close to sharing my body with a man on a picnic blanket this afternoon any more than I did. And you know something, Darik, we could have done that. I'm certain of it. But right now isn't the right time and we both know it."

"If you don't mind an awkward question," he asked, "when did you decide I might be the kind of man you'd be interested in?"

"At the gun shop. As soon as you walked in. You had this glow surrounding you, something special, and I absolutely believed my guardian angel brought you to Pueblo with a purpose in mind."

"Which was?"

"To be a friend, first of all. Most of all. Someone who could help me release the pain from my husband's death. He died before we ever made love, before we even spent a night together. His heart stopped for no reason at the wedding. We were dancing, laughing, and having so much fun," she said as tears streamed down her cheeks. "He lifted me high into the air and spun around as everyone was singing and shouting, and then we fell to the ground. At first I thought he'd slipped or his knee buckled or he was kidding around. Everyone thought it was a joke at first. But I looked at his face as we lay on the ground and knew he was gone. He died just like that."

"I'm so sorry. I'm not making small talk, but I've lost both of the women I've loved. One in a fire, my true love I guess you'd call her. The other woman, my wife and the mother of my daughter, she died from consumption. I understand how you feel; at least I know how I felt. It's hell. Impossible to explain to someone who hasn't gone through it."

They stroked one another's hands with long, tender motions. She placed her index finger on his lips and asked, "Were you with one of them just now while I was fixing lunch? Maybe both? Don't fret. I won't be mad if that's what was happening."

He stared into her eyes without saying a word.

"Darik, I'll be completely honest. I closed my eyes when you walked up to the pond, and all I could see was Chad, my husband, not you. We were married just a few hours, but he was my husband, and I'm sure he was my one true love. I'm romantic by nature and know for a certainty that he was the one. Never have been sure if I'd let another man come into my life. I hope you're not angry. It just happened. I didn't plan things this way. In so many ways, I want to be with you, and I figured a picnic was a good way to find out who you really are and what makes you special. But here we are with one another, and I find myself wanting to be with him as though he never died. Does that make sense? I hope you don't hate me."

He smiled. "I've been around. I've been with plenty of woman… in that way. But I've only really made love to two women in my life who I actually loved. Not proud of it and not ashamed of it. One was Lihua. She died two days after the only time we were together as lovers. But we'd made a promise to find a way to be together forever, and then she died in a fire. Just like that. I've still not gotten over her death. I know I haven't. The other woman, Ingrid, was my wife. She was your age when we met. She was a virgin until we got married, and that was long after Lihua died.

Ingrid saved my life. She gave me a kind of love and abiding friendship that was new to me. She was a good wife and a wonderful mother. But we were only together for a few years before she took ill, and then I had to watch her fade away into nothing but memories."

"Who were you with…I mean, when I came out of the pond?" Vida asked. "Is that too nosy? If it is, don't answer. Did you feel like you were in two places at the same time? Maybe more than two? That's what it felt like to me. I was with you entirely as you walked toward me at the pond. Then suddenly you became Chad. And then you became you again. And even though my body was here, my heart and mind were going back and forth. I'm embarrassed that it happened. But you know what, I've never spoken with a man like this before, not like this. As a rule I'm very private, but this is how I've imagined two best friends might talk with each other. Society doesn't make it easy for a man and a woman to be friends and so open if they're not married. I like it."

"New to me too," he replied. "But don't ever be embarrassed about who you are or for what we're doing today, you know… speaking so honestly," Darik replied. "You're an angel. It feels like you were sent to help me finally say goodbye to them both. I was in love twice but not at the same time. In Sedona, I learned that time, what we call time, is something we create out of thin air kind of like how we store things in a pantry. We box up time in order to keep things organized. But the longer I've been on this ride from Tejada, the more I realized that I need to live fully wherever I am. And the living has to take place inside me. It's not back in Romania. It's not in a pile of ashes near Denver. It's not in Louviers, Castle Rock, Tejada, Sedona, and not in Pueblo. Those are just places on a map. I'm talking about living within myself."

She nodded but remained silent.

"I'm trying to be alive wherever I am. That's not something I've done very well. And from now on, no matter the time of day, the day itself, the month or the year, none of that matters anymore. This is all temporary—what we see, what we taste, and maybe even what we think we might believe. For me, recognizing this is the way I'm finally escaping the sadness I've worn around my collar like barbed wire all these years, maybe my entire life. And I'm sharing these feelings with someone I trust. We're sharing the feelings and also making memories that can make us feel better later. I'm not the smartest man in the world, but this is what I think a good life is all about. Sure, I've got to earn money to pay for room and board, to buy tools to carve the birdhouses, clothes and things like that. But…"

She smiled and interrupted abruptly, "But did you have time to carve a birdhouse for my father? If not, I won't be angry. What we're doing right now, this conversation, is more important than any birdhouse you could carve. Father doesn't know about your birdhouses unless Gurneath or the gunsmith bumped into him, so whether you carved one for him doesn't really matter, especially since I have a hunch you'll be on the trail again pretty quickly. I'll get him something else if I have to."

Darik stood, walked over to his saddlebag, and pulled from it an object wrapped in white muslin. He sat down next to her, kissed her gently on the forehead, and handed it to her. She unrolled the muslin and gasped when she saw the birdhouse. She placed her right hand on Darik's cheek and took a deep breath, slowly exhaling, saying nothing.

She examined every aspect of the birdhouse, rubbing her fingers over the four animal heads carved into its exterior. "You amaze me. What you've made and what you've shared with me today—all of it is amazing. I don't know what to say other than 'thank you.' I know it's not enough, not even close, but thank you."

He took the object from her, set it down on the muslin, then propped himself up on his left his elbow and stared into her eyes as though they held the answer to everything.

"I was with Lihua at the same time I was with you," he said, "by the pond and just now. And for a few moments, I was also with Ingrid, but her image faded away pretty fast. Lihua took ownership of my heart the minute I first saw her. It ain't meant to offend you, but I've never gotten over her. Guess you can tell. Never grieved honestly about losing her and never knew how to let go. Ingrid was a fine woman; in fact, she was elegant and wise for her age. She knew I loved her, but she always knew Lihua couldn't be replaced in my heart, mostly because I wouldn't let her be. I felt poorly whenever I gave it much thought, but I was true to Ingrid because she knew my story, all my stories, and let me be myself. In fact, she encouraged it. She knew I would stand by her and our daughter for as long as I lived. She tolerated me being so confused."

"I know what that feels like. I was trapped in my grief," Vida replied. "Wouldn't let myself be near any of the suitors who thought they could replace Chad. And trust me, with a caring father and four protective brothers, a suitor had to be on his best behavior just to get an invitation to our dinner table."

"I can believe that," he said with a laugh. "If your father and brothers are half as determined as you, it'd be quite the task to measure up."

"You would, Darik. You'd measure up fine. In a lot of ways, I think you'd be the perfect man for me. You'd be the perfect new son for my father and the perfect new brother for my brothers. But your journey isn't ending here. I know it and you know it. You've got a daughter, one I imagine to be as beautiful as any child on Earth, and I'll bet she's wondering when you're coming back to her."

"Yep. I have to head back to Tejada. Theresa's lost her mother and has a father who's been riding in circles for months. I'd stay here forever if my life wasn't so damn complicated."

"Everyone's life is complicated, Darik. But the gift of a child of your own and the gift of being in love twice is something most people never get."

"Three times now, at least it's beginning to feel that way. In love three times, all different from one another."

She leaned forward and placed her mouth upon his as lightly as possible. They kissed, she stroked his cheek as he stroked hers, and they rose from the blanket and went their separate ways, Vida in her buckboard, Darik on his horse.

Several carpenters without any tools were using their bare hands to build a gazebo made of white wood, a structure that resembled marble but behaved like pliable clay able to be reshaped with little effort. Although the work was still underway, the structure began floating in a lily pond the size of the corral at Eagle Trail Ranch. There were no ladders nor scaffolding, yet the men working on the gazebo were able to reach all parts of the structure simply by extending their arms far beyond their normal reach.

He was in a small rowboat tied to the gazebo which now appeared to be sitting atop a river barge. The workmen had all vanished. Sitting on a bench in the gazebo was a young girl who held a small doll in her hands. The girl's face was covered by a thin veil, light blue in color. Her green eyes shone through brightly. Several men walking on the outer edge of the large barge encircled the gazebo, moving up and down like hand-carved horses on a merry-go-round. The girl was engrossed in a discussion with the red-headed doll and paid little attention to everything else.

CHAPTER 19
Resurrection

Darik stopped off at the Eagle Trail Ranch on his ride to Denver with the intention of keeping his visit brief, no more than a few hours. As it turned out, he stayed the night after enjoying a festive meal and too many shots of locally-distilled whiskey with Mulroony and Silvano, both of whom now behaved more like friends of Darik's than his former bosses.

Until Darik shared details about his life since his disappearance five years earlier, neither had been aware of his involvement, brief as it was, with a Chinese woman, Lihua, nor did they know much about the fire at Mrs. Brown's property. They were surprised to learn of his move to Castle Rock where he settled down with another young woman, and both men expressed whiskey-influenced sadness when he described her death.

"I'm confused, Darik. I kind of understand you feeling so sad after losing both women, but why the hell aren't you back home with your daughter?" Mulroony asked. "Why in blazes are you back here? She's your daughter."

Silvano nodded in agreement in between pouring whiskey into his shot glass multiple times.

"Some unfinished business, personal stuff that I have to take care of. I'll be back home with Theresa in no time at all," he responded.

"I think you're wasting valuable time, son, but that's your decision— not mine or Silvano's. Just take care of things and go home. Having a family and all that comes with it isn't something to risk, especially with a child who's already lost one of her parents. I'd think you'd be more concerned about your daughter not having you around for so long."

Darik stared. "You're right. I know you're right. But like I said, there's just one thing I need to take care of, and I can only get it done in Denver. Then I'm heading back to Tejada. Hell, I might take the train down to Trinidad and shave a couple weeks off my return trip. I'll just have to wait and see."

Darik avoided sharing anything about the night on the Sedona ledge with Fierce Night Sky because he was unsure of how to explain it in a context that the inebriated men would understand. When he began explaining the encounter he had in Pueblo with Vida, he lied and told the men that it occurred in a small village near the Arizona border, and he changed her name to Darleen just in case either man knew her family.

Most of the whiskey-laden discussion was about Darik finally coming to terms with the tragic losses he had experienced beginning in his infancy, and how he had come to believe that most everything in life, at least his own, only had a fragile, temporary quality to it.

"Don't know how to explain things clearly," he said, "but I'm learning to take hold of each moment in my life and cope better with all the shit that seems to come hand in hand with living…no matter how we plan things out."

Mulroony and Silvano remained silent. Darik got the impression that they were glad to see he had grown up, but he also sensed they were still disappointed he had not spoken to them about his sudden decision to leave the ranch and move to Castle Rock five years earlier.

A little after sunrise and following only four hours of sleep, Darik attached his large cantle bag to the back of his saddle and tied off the small case containing his tools on the opposite side of the saddle from his saddle bag. He then began the short ride to Denver, veering slightly toward Mrs. Brown's property north of Bear Creek.

As he approached the familiar land, he noticed that the house had been completely rebuilt, this time in red brick and large, multi-colored stones, although the lower portion of the new structure was composed of gray granite. Several children, all Chinese from what he could tell, none of whom appeared older than nine or ten, were running around in the yard, but he had no desire to venture any closer.

He dismounted and walked his horse through the same grove of trees along the creek where he first saw Lihua. He approached the cottonwood where he mounted the birdhouse five years earlier, now an adult tree well over four feet in circumference. The birdhouse was now situated high above the ground.

His intention was to place a love note inside the birdhouse, something he had written a year after Lihua died, only a few months before he married Ingrid. As he pulled up alongside the tree, he realized that even by standing atop his saddle he would have to shimmy up a few feet to reach the birdhouse.

With the folded note in his vest pocket so it would be easy to retrieve once he reached the birdhouse, he began climbing.

He was awestruck by the spectacular view of the foothills and the familiar western horizon that remained lined with snowcapped peaks far into the back country. When he was head high with the opening to the birdhouse, he reached into his vest pocket with one hand while with the other hand he held onto the birdhouse which he thought had become an inseparable part of the tree trunk.

His grip on the birdhouse faltered slightly as he pulled out the letter from his pocket, and this caused him to drop the love note. He instinctively grabbed for the falling paper, but in doing so he pulled on the birdhouse with such force that the screws gave way, and he began falling to the ground while looking directly into the oval shaped opening on the front of the birdhouse only an inch from his face. His head glanced off the side of the saddle, just above the left stirrup, and he landed on the ground with such impact that he was knocked unconscious as the birdhouse grazed his cheek just below his right eye. Blood flowed out in a steady stream. Unconscious and with his mouth wide open, he began choking on his own blood. He reacted instinctively by turning his head sideways as he regained consciousness, but he had little strength to spit the warm, acidic tasting blood out of his mouth.

"Mister! Mister! You alive?" he heard a child's voice shouting. "Don't move. You alive, mister?"

He wiped blood from his eyelids and found himself staring into the face of a terrified young girl no older than six. "Not quite sure, Missy. Let me figure out what just happened, and then I'll tell you if I'm alive or not."

"You fell. I watched. You climbed up to that birdhouse and then fell with it in your hand until you let go of it. But then it hit you in the face. I thought you died."

"Missy, remind yourself to never do what I just did. Don't climb trees. Not at all. Especially tall ones. It's not safe. Where's the birdhouse?"

"Over here. I'll get it for you," she replied.

"That's fine. No rush. I can't hold anything just yet. Did it break?"

"No. Not broken. Just a little blood on the corner where it hit you. Built strong, that's for sure."

He laughed. "Yep, glad to know it didn't break. I carved it myself a long time ago. Even put it on that tree. I didn't really mean to pull it down. I had something else in mind."

"What?"

"Oh," he replied in a melancholy tone, "it doesn't really matter a whole lot now. Not sure how I'll ever get it back up there."

"Find another tree," she suggested with a laugh, "a shorter one, one you can reach and attach the birdhouse. Then watch the tree grow. And before you know it, the birdhouse will be on top of another tall tree just like it was before you tore it down."

"You're one smart young lady, aren't you?"

"I can read and write. I can read the words on the top of the birdhouse, too. How'd they get there?"

"I carved them."

"Pretty. I know someone with that name."

"Which one?" he asked.

"Lihua. Very Chinese. Did you know that? Many Chinese women have that name."

"That so? Live and learn. I thought it was unique to her. Do you know what unique means?"

The girl shook her head. "What does it mean?"

He thought about the best way to describe it, all the while considering the similarity of the little girl's facial features to Lihua. "Something that is the only one of its kind. That make sense?"

"I think so."

"What's your name?"

"Mei. Short for Mei Ling. Want me to spell it?"

"Sure."

"Capital m. Then e. Then i. And then a second word that starts with capital L, an i, then a small n, and then a small g. Mei Ling."

"Very good. I figured it was M-a-y like the month."

"My favorite month. I was born in May. But my name means *beautiful and delicate* in Chinese. Does not mean the month."

"You're Chinese?"

"My mother was Chinese. She died. I do not know my father. I was born here at Mrs. Brown's. I am American but also Chinese. Sometimes confusing."

"I'll bet. I was born in another country and moved to America when I was young. I used to get confused too. Am I still bleeding? I took quite a knock to the face."

"Not bleeding, but it is an ugly cut. I do not think you should move. Maybe you broke bones?"

Darik had been conducting a limb by limb inventory as they spoke, and though he had yet to stand, he was confident that no bones were broken. "Thanks for caring so much, Mei Ling, but I'm okay."

She laughed. "Maybe you should come to Mrs. Brown's house and have someone fix the cut."

He nodded in agreement. "Let me get to my feet, and then we'll see about walking over there."

His horse had been standing motionless since the fall, and Darik thought, just for a moment, that the animal had winked at him to acknowledge that the injury was not severe. Then again, he thought the fall and minor head injury might have created that illusion. Slowly, as he regained his balance and with the horse's reins in hand, he and Mei Ling walked toward the large brick home on the site where Lihua had been burned to death.

"Whatcha got there, young lady? Looks like a bloody cowboy," commented a woman in a formal looking dress.

"Bad fall, Mrs. Brown. He fell off a tree. Says no broken bones. Ugly cut on his face. See?"

Darik tipped his hat in a courteous manner. "Sorry to intrude, Mrs. Brown, but this youngster says my face is in need of some assistance although the bleeding has stopped. What's your opinion?"

"You look familiar as hell, Cowboy. Doesn't matter. She's right. Mei Ling usually is. Yes, sir, that's quite a cut, but not too deep. How about you set yourself down, and I'll get one of the gals to clean you up. Don't need any stitches. Let's clean you up and see what's under all that."

"Thank you, ma'am. I'm not meaning to barge in and disrupt anything. Much obliged for your help."

She smiled and walked toward the back door to her house. She turned after a few steps. "I never forget a face. I'll figure you out soon enough. Give me a few minutes. Now just stay put. Be right back."

An elderly Chinese woman accompanied Mrs. Brown back to the table where Darik and Mei Ling were chatting. She carried a small basket containing bandages and a few other items. She was no taller than five feet but had a dominating presence. She leaned within inches of his face to examine the wound, dabbed the cut with a strong smelling liquid poured from a bottle she took from the basket, used some soft cloth to pat it dry, and then applied a stinging, aromatic ointment.

"Whoa! What is that stuff?" he asked in a loud voice. "Appreciate the help, but that hurts worse than the fall."

Mei Ling laughed. "You're not so tough. Not so tough. It's medicine she makes from trees and flowers. They have a lot of secrets and she understands them."

He smiled. "I know a lot about trees, Mei Ling, more than you can imagine. That's why I carve birdhouses. It's as though the trees give me permission to carve the birdhouses, something I've been doing since I was about your age back home. Kind of hard to explain, but it's just something I'm glad I'm able to do."

Mrs. Brown's accommodating tone suddenly shifted to a terseness that surprised Darik. "Mei, he's from a faraway place called Romania. Far across the ocean."

The look in Mrs. Brown's eyes had transformed into an angry stare as though she knew more than she was saying. Darik took note as she glared. "What's on your mind, Mrs. Brown? Looks like you want to ask me something."

"No, not really. Something tells me we've never been formally introduced, but I think we know each other. Don't we? That happens now and then. You know, never get introduced but know a hell of a lot about a stranger. Ever have that happen, cowboy?"

He smiled. "Yes, you're right. You and I were never introduced. I came by here the day of the fire. Just briefly. I'm glad to see you built such a fine new house. Looks like this one will withstand almost anything."

"Might stand up to weather," she replied, "but not to a broken heart." She turned and walked to the back door at a rapid pace. "Mei Ling, you and Shu need to come inside. The cowboy ain't gonna bleed to death. He can get back on his horse and ride to wherever he's headed this time. No need to say goodbye or thanks. Not his style."

Mei Ling stood, shook hands with Darik as he bowed his head slightly. "Thank you, Mei Ling. Very sweet of you to help me. I should get going. Still have to ride into Denver before dark. Please thank the other lady for tending to my cut. I'll be gone. Take care."

He had not replied to Mrs. Brown as she walked away and he got on his horse. His eyes were focused on the rangeland separating Mrs. Brown's property from Denver itself, a few miles to the northeast.

Hank Fisher

A small bonfire burned in the distance near a lush meadow surrounded by flowering trees, species he had never seen nor imagined. The smell of the bonfire seemed to be enhanced by fist-sized blossoms appearing in royal purples, crimson reds, golden yellows, and sapphire blue. His view was from treetop level and the terrain was unfamiliar. A couple of small farmhouses, bright red ones, were adjacent to a large barn the size of a hill at least fifty or sixty feet tall. A huge wooden fence surrounding the corral, nearly as high as the barn, blocked him in every direction as he was suddenly standing on the ground.

CHAPTER 20
Fraternity

On Darik's third morning in Denver, he again awakened at sunrise in a boarding house a mile walk from the site of the new state capitol building. He felt rested after another night's sleep on a mattress, actually a six-inch pad of horse blankets covered by one thin sheet that kept the itch to a minimum. It was certainly more accommodating to his body than the hard ground he had gotten accustomed to during the past several weeks riding the trails other than a few nights at Gurneath's rooming house in Pueblo.

The smell of fresh coffee brewing in the kitchen floated up to his room. He came downstairs and saw the landlady's cook preparing steak and eggs for Darik and several other male tenants residing in the sixteen-room, three-story wooden framed building.

Despite thinking he would only stop briefly in Denver, instead he decided to stay in a rooming house for two weeks to sort things out further. He took a temporary job at a wood mill located a mile northwest from the boarding house. The foreman only wanted last names, so Darik was known only as "Jacoby." No one knew his first name.

Denver was a boom town and his carpentry experience was being rewarded by the mill's owner with a salary of two dollars a day for ten-hour shifts. The boarding house cost him four dollars a week, and it included a hot bath and breakfast each day. It was not inexpensive, but the extra money made from selling birdhouses to Gurneath had brought the total in his pocket to one hundred and fifty dollars. While he was only earning a few dollars each day, it was more than enough to keep him comfortable during this part of a journey that now had no real purpose since he had reclaimed the birdhouse with his and Lihua's names carved on top.

Darik spent his off hours working on new birdhouses, foregoing visits to nearby taverns or the brothels in walking distance from his room. During his first two weeks in Denver, he had roughed out six new birdhouses from medium-sized blocks of pine he took from the scrap pile at the mill at no cost. Each birdhouse was slightly larger than the one he carved for Vida, and he figured he could charge as much as eight dollars to a shop owner interested in selling them at retail for at least twelve dollars.

The modernization of Denver during his five-year absence was striking. The city had further shed its persona as a wild cattle and mining town and had grown into one of the largest cities in the West.

Countless small office buildings and shops, numerous boarding houses, hotels of varying quality, and dozens of beautiful Victorian homes on all sides of the modernized downtown Denver now filled new neighborhoods that had sprung up. No matter which direction he traveled from Union Station, which was only a quarter mile from his boarding house, the city showed signs that it had evolved from a cow town into a significant center of commerce. The new public cemetery was a half mile south and slightly east of the Capitol, a twenty-minute horseback ride for Darik, who could not figure out why it was not built on the flatlands five miles further east since wealthy citizens would eventually not want to live so close to it.

His mind meandered as he explored the city. He wondered if he had changed as much as Denver or if it was just his shifting perspectives. He speculated about whether Mrs. Brown and Lihua had spoken about him during the forty-eight hours that elapsed between those powerful moments he shared with her and the fatal fire. If so, he wondered if Mrs. Brown despised him for taking Lihua's virginity or if Lihua had even told her. He also thought about his grandparents and considered whether his grandfather would approve of the birdhouses he was now creating.

Darik finished breakfast and decided to take a walking tour of the busiest streets in the neighborhood since he did not have to report to the mill for another two hours.

"What's in the saddlebag, son?" a bespectacled man bald as an eagle's egg asked while stepping down from the ladder he was using to reach the upper shelves in the first store Darik entered. "It's bulging like it's going to have twins."

"Something I'd consider selling if you think any of your customers might be interested in artwork," Darik replied in a dignified and confident tone.

"Hold on! Skip the bullshit. This is a fucking mercantile, not an art gallery in Paris. What is it you want to say?"

Darik chuckled. "I carve birdhouses. Better than anything around here. Some say best in the country. I've been carving them for more than fifteen years. Want to take a look?"

"Fifteen years? Now you're just bullshitting me, son. You ain't old enough to have been doing much more than sucking your mama's tit fifteen years ago. Am I right?"

Darik, still somewhat baby-faced at age twenty-eight, glared and tried to keep his composure. "I worked at the Eagle Trail Ranch in Littleton for nine years. Started there when I was fourteen. I've been gone for five years. But honestly, mister, do I look like some kid who's never taken a woman to bed or gotten drunk in a bar? Do you want to look at the carvings or just sound like a jackass?"

"Eagle Trail? I know the place," the man said. "Sold a lot of stuff to Mulroony when he used to shop in town. That's a long time ago. I remember when his wife died. Tore him up for quite a while. What'd you do out there?"

"Anything I was asked. I'm good with horses and know how to work cattle. Most the time I did the carpentry and fixed stuff. Built the new barn and mess hall and did a lot of the work on Mulroony's house and the bunk house where I lived. I'm damn good at it too. Any other questions?"

The man held out his hand and said, "Okay, kid, you got me. I just get pissed when salesmen walk in trying to sell me everything under the sun as though I'm some sort of idiot. Hell, I know what I want to buy, and I base it on what I know will sell. That being said, let's take a look at your birdhouses. Birdhouses? Goddamn birdhouses, you say?"

Darik unwrapped the muslin covering the six new birdhouses, each one displaying different ornamental details including starbursts, lightning bolts, horse heads and pine trees. Each was larger than Vida's, and he also provided long, high quality screws for mounting, three per birdhouse.

"Well, goddamn!" he exclaimed. "They're not birdhouses. You're right, they're art. This stuff should be in a museum. I wouldn't think of letting a sparrow crap in one of these. Way too nice looking. What kind of wood? Pine?"

"Yep. Pine. And I don't paint them. I use a special oil I mix myself that I learned about in Romania from my grandfather. I rub it in to give them an expensive looking sheen. They'll stand up to a dozen winters, probably twice that amount if they're mounted correctly on a tree or the side of building. If you think one of your customers might want one for a parlor room or office, then I'd be glad to make stands for them."

"How much?"

"With or without the stands? Don't have any stands made just yet. Might take me a couple days."

"How much you want?"

"Ten dollars as is. I'd do twelve with a stand. If you buy stands for all six in the bag, I'd do eleven each. Sixty-six dollars total."

The older man laughed. "Son, you know as much about numbers as you do about wood; at least that's how it's lookin' to me. You already had this figured out before you walked in the door, didn't you?"

Darik smiled. "Yep. I'd been told you're a good businessman and that I needed to be thinking on my feet. How'd I do?"

Extending his hand out to Darik, he said, "Deal. But I'll pay you nine each for the six as is, no stands. Fifty-four dollars. I can sell them for thirteen, maybe a bit higher. Hell, if someone wants a stand, I'll have them talk to you directly. You can charge them whatever you want. Keeps my costs down, and I don't have to figure out where to store them. How's that sound?"

"Works for me. I'm Darik. Darik Jacoby."

"Pere is mine. Foster Pere. Pappy opened his first general store here in 1860, the year after gold was discovered over there where Cherry Creek and the Platte meet up. Know the place?"

"Sure do. That's on the route I followed riding into town."

"I built this store in seventy-five, the year before statehood. Figured someday Denver'd have an elegant Main Street, probably by the train station, and that's why my store's right here. I own the whole block. The other four storefronts are renters, and since I also own the corner bar, let's make this official and I'll buy you a drink?"

"Sure. But only coffee."

"That's up to you. Drink whatever you want. It'll be on me."

After Pere examined each birdhouse, commenting favorably about the degree of detail, he walked to the front door, turned the hanging placard to "CLOSED," and pulled the door shut as he and Darik headed across the wooden planked sidewalk.

"Pretty wobbly but not too bad," Darik commented as he looked down at the weather-worn wooden sidewalk. "I could build you a better sidewalk than this. Lots better. This one ain't going to last too long. Already coming apart. Those are awfully thin planks and they weren't installed properly. Not at all. Second rate construction."

"This fucking sidewalk was built by some son of a bitch the mayor had in his back pocket a few years back, or maybe it's the other way around. The bastard who owns the mill on the far side of the tracks built all of the downtown sidewalks and they're shabby as hell."

Darik chuckled. "That's where I work."

"Seriously?"

"Yeah. It's the truth. I started there when I came to town two weeks ago. Want me to see about getting my boss to let me come over and fix it so it'll last? Won't be good for your business if someone breaks a leg when one of these planks busts up. Your other choice is for me to just fix things up in my spare time and not let him know. That way he wouldn't charge you for any work I do."

"You get that done for me on your own, and I'll raise the price to ten dollars each. That'd be sixty dollars. Lot of money for birdhouses. Hope they sell fast. Hate putting out that much cash on a hunch."

"Tell you what. Any that don't sell in two weeks, I'll buy 'em back at the same price so you won't be stuck with extra inventory."

"Why would you make that offer?"

"Truth is, I'll make you a bet, and let's make it another dollar just for fun, that all six are sold within a week. If that happens, you owe me an extra dollar for each. Okay?"

"I'm not much of a gambling man. Truth is that I don't believe these will be on the shelf more than three days. Let's skip the bet. I'm a man of honor or try to be. I said ten dollars each if you fix the sidewalk. Let's shake on it!"

For the next couple of hours, the two men found themselves in a straightforward conversation about their personal lives, something more typical of lifelong friends than virtual strangers. Darik recounted his arrival in Colorado after leaving Romania, working at the cattle ranch, parts of the story about Lihua and the fire at Mrs. Brown's as well as Ingrid's death and his daughter living with Lynetta in Tejada.

Pere remembered the fire although he had not seen it in person. "Was told it was mighty explosive and that the place didn't burn more than thirty minutes before nothing but the chimney stack was left. Couple of people got killed. Chinese. Yep. Too bad one was your girlfriend. You must have felt miserable. No wonder you left. But to tell you the truth, the way most people around here hate the Chinese, no respect for them at all, I think you'd have found yourself in a heap of trouble by being with her in a public sort of way or trying to settle down with her. Sorry to say that, but I know how people behave around here, particularly one Irishman who runs the opium den and whorehouse next to the train station. Chinese are just slaves to him. Cattle and horses get more respect than the Chinese get here. Your lady friend must have been quite the looker for you to risk it. But that's how a man's heart behaves. I ought to know; my own father was French and he loved beautiful women, poetry, and fine paintings. I think it's part of French blood to be so caught up in love and art."

"Never gave a second thought to her being Chinese," Darik replied. "I'm as much a foreigner as she was. It's just not easy to see I'm not from around here. Definitely lots easier for me to fit in than for the Indians, Chinese, and the black men and women, and the Mexicans too. They can't hide from their birthright. It's right there on their faces for everyone to see."

"Darik, listen to me," Pere commented between sips of his beer, "almost no adults are from here. Not really from here. Hardly a fucking soul. Not the senators, not the governor, not the mayor, not the beer makers, not the big gold mining companies, and not Bonfils or Tammen over at the newspaper. I'm one of the few men my age actually born here, and I'm definitely not a big-time socialite like Mrs. Brown, that old whore, or the family that owns the brewery up in Golden. None of them are from here. With few exceptions the only people who were born here are the Utes, Kiowa, Sioux, Arapahoe, Pawnee, and the other Indians who used to spend the winters camped over near Cherry Creek or along lower Bear Creek or Clear Creek and a few of the other streams. As far as I'm concerned, everyone else is a foreigner. Doesn't mean I don't like them, the carpetbaggers who keep coming in with big money; it just means that newcomers don't always have the same regard for local traditions as those of us whose roots are actually here.

"Listen, Darik, I could give a shit where you're from—where anyone's from!" he said in a louder voice as he emptied the last of the beer. "Hell, whether a guy's Catholic, Baptist, Jewish, or he's Chinese or a Mexican or a Romanian or wherever the hell you just said you're from, I don't care. Not at all.

"Denver's going to become a real city someday. Maybe not in my lifetime, but it'll be huge. No city between Kansas City and San Francisco will be bigger. I guarantee it. I just want to make sure it grows up the right way. We need people to settle here who come from other places. We need people with new ideas who want to create new businesses and who might bring in some sort of culture that'll overcome the hateful bastards you'll meet. I got my motives. I'm someone who's got property and wants to make money. Who doesn't? I want to make enough money to live the rest my life as comfortably as possible, and so does everyone else who's come here. And, hell, Darik, the people who've gotten treated like garbage since day one are the natives, the Indians. Everything they ever owned has been stolen by the whites, especially by the government, including our local politicians and the military. They've been murdered and beaten without anyone getting punished. They get bothered all day and night by drunk cowboys and landowners. And the sheriff and police hate them. Hell, I'm just glad nobody can look at me and know where my kin came from. Like you, I can blend in. Practically invisible."

"So it doesn't make any difference that I'm a Jew from Romania?"

"What part didn't you get? I don't care about that, and I could care less that you're a Jew. I never bought into religion or praying to some sort of holy ghost. What I care about is that when someone tells me something that I'm not getting smothered in bullshit. Be straight with me and you'll get the same back. As for where someone might have been born or if they're so weak that they have to have to pray for forgiveness, it's just not something I understand. Not at all."

Darik stared into his eyes. "You said some guy from Ireland runs the opium den and whorehouse nearby. How'd that happen? How come the Chinese don't? That's where the opium comes from, the Orient. Why don't they run their own businesses?"

"Too much money involved. Big profits. Money drives everything here. And as long as there's white men in charge of government, the police and the banks, nothing's going to change. Besides, it ain't legal for the Chinese to own any bars or whorehouses here, not yet, but I think the laws will change since the bankers and their investors want money and don't care where it comes from or what color skin is handing it over. Pretty clear that these bankers believe that being crooked and selling drugs and whores is a freedom that should be available to all people whether the color of their skin is yellow, brown, black, or white."

Darik nodded. This was not the kind of discussion he anticipated when he first walked into the mercantile. He had never met someone as knowledgeable about such a wide range of subjects as Pere nor anyone with such outspoken opinions. Other than Mulroony and Silvano, he had never discussed being Jewish with anyone else since he arrived in America even though it meant little to him these days. While being a Jew was only a small part of his life in Romania, he saw no real value in being Jewish once he reached America although he had no explanation for his feelings.

"Politicians, bankers, and crooks," Pere continued, "one and the same—white men with power. They want control over everything—what's legal and what ain't. And the illegal businesses are fine for them because that's where the big profits are. Not in a shop like mine. Small stuff. But selling pussy and opium, that's big money. And like me, they also realize owning land is essential to being prosperous in the future."

Darik listened in silence.

"Even my bar," Pere continued, "and I do all right selling beer and whiskey, but I don't make a fraction of the profit at the bar compared to even the smallest of the opium dens. Not even close. And these days it's that fucking Irishman who's in charge and not the Italians on the far north side of the Platte up in the highlands above the river nor the Polish or Germans in the stockyards where the Platte flows out of town."

"I don't know enough about Denver to know who's in charge. I had no clue," Darik responded.

"My grandparents were French and my pappy was raised in France. But he was adventurous. He left there at eighteen and eventually made his way to America. Thought he'd become a trapper. Must have seemed like a romantic profession, at least until he met a young woman from Germany on the wagon train from New York, a trip that took nearly five months back then. He married her during the trip, and they settled down in these parts a few years before gold was found.

"There was nothing out here. And I mean nothing. He told me that other than the mountains to the west, this was a wasteland as flat as Kansas and Oklahoma, and not nearly as lush as Nebraska. I was born in my parents' bed. Not long after that my mother took sick and died. Just died. Years later he told me that it was then when he decided there was more money to be made from a general merchandise store and being a landman than working his ass off as a trapper or farmer.

"He made a plan and set out to buy as much property around Denver as he could afford. He followed through on his plan a little at a time and he did well. He bought and sold land right up 'til he died a decade ago. I still buy and sell land. That's where

I make my real money. The store keeps me in a perfect position to hear about who's doing this and who's doing that. Listening is how a good landman can make a fortune."

"So you're French? Never met a Frenchman before."

"Still haven't. I'm from here, like I said, one of the rare ones, a native. Born and raised spitting distance from this very table. I don't speak a word of French. Pappy wanted me and my little brother to be American. English only; no French in the house except for him and what little he might have taught my mother before she died in 1853. I was born in 1852. That makes me thirty-six, so please don't call me an 'old timer' again. I'm not a lot older than you. Pappy got married again a few years later and then my brother was born. Then his second wife died. Hell, poor man was grieving for years and had to raise me and my brother by himself."

"I still speak Romanian," Darik said changing the subject, "but nobody else in these parts can. But I'm rusty after fifteen years of only speaking English. Too bad. It's beautiful. And even though Lihua was Chinese, she only spoke in English around me. Very slowly. Did it nice."

"You got snagged by that woman real fast. Pretty obvious you're still carrying a heavy heart. I'd like to have met her to see what it was that was so special. Maybe in my next lifetime I'll be lucky enough to make her acquaintance," Pere said with a grin.

"Next lifetime? You believe that stuff? Thought you didn't believe in religion?"

"Never felt strongly about what I believe or don't when it comes to religion. I don't pray. It's a joke. Never cared what others believe in or pray about. I know what I know. I have faith, but it's mostly in myself and those few folks I trust. Sure, I rely on myself most the time and own up to the decisions I make. I hope I'm honest about what I think is true. But believing too strongly in something outside one's own absolute sense of what's right and what's wrong is what leads to war and the butchery of slavery and the mistreatment of the Indians, the Chinese, and the Mexicans. Most people are too attached to their religious beliefs. I'm all for having some sort of moral compass as some might say, but it's got to be in a man's heart. I never believed in a religion or in some grouchy white-haired god up in the clouds or a son of a bitch in hell. It seems like religion's a way to not accept responsibility for the awful things we humans have been doing to each other since the beginning of time—if there was actually a beginning. I tend to think life just exists, and it didn't take a god or invisible power to create all this. Those churchgoing folks are always saying, 'It's god's will,' depending on which god someone claims is the only true one. It's crap and I hate it! You're either someone who owns up to what they do for themselves and to others, or you're a fool and a liar. There's no in between."

Darik smiled, still trying to comprehend Foster Pere's streetwise nature and no-nonsense personality, which was not that of a criminal nor con artist; at least it did not appear so at this early juncture in what Darik sensed could become a friendship. He had never experienced a close friend in all the years he lived in Colorado and had become even more isolated and untrusting of most other people since he relocated to New Mexico with Ingrid and Lynetta.

"I ought to get going. The foreman at the mill has some repair work in the main building I have to tend to. Thanks for the coffee, Pere. Nice to make your acquaintance. I'll bring the birdhouses back over tomorrow. Want to clean 'em up and make sure they're perfect."

"Fair enough. Appreciate the gesture. Tell me one thing though. Everyone I know who has a special something, whether it's cooking, fishing, working with masonry, or, hell, even some old woman who makes quilts—all of you artistic types have a secret, some sort of treasured piece or bit of information that you don't share. You that way? You got a birdhouse that's the best you ever made that's hidden away?"

Darik nodded. "Sure. One really special one. Got it here in the other side of the saddlebag. Hold on. I'll go get it." When he returned to the bar and uncovered the birdhouse he had made for Lihua, Pere's eyes grew huge.

"Now that's something special! Best of the bunch. Really detailed. And I like the carving of the names on top. Better than any romantic love song a cowboy'd sing to his lady, even a French cowboy," he said with a grin. "What's the plan for this one? And what's the red stuff on the corner? That blood?"

"Yep. Smacked me in the forehead a few days ago when I got careless. Mounted it on the tree I mentioned. Did it for Lihua nearly five years ago. But I yanked it down from the tree when I fell. I'm going to sand out the blood stain and put on another coating of oil. After that, I'm not sure. Probably just keep it as a reminder. Not sure."

"Tell you what. Fix it up however you want and I'll put it in the main display case. It'll get lots of attention. I won't sell it. Hell, when someone sees those names carved on top, their imaginations will run wild since most people like to copy the ideas of others instead of inventing their own. I'll bet someone'll want their own name carved on their birdhouse for a personal keepsake. You could charge more for doing it. Would you do that?"

He shrugged his shoulders. "Don't know. Hadn't thought about it. This was a one-time thing I did with Lihua. Not sure anyone else would want names carved. Whatcha think?"

"Oh, they would. If not a name, maybe a proverb or something from the Bible, silly as that seems. Hell, I don't know. Looks like you could carve a love letter on the birdhouse, a little on each wall and the roof. Could you?"

"I could but don't know about engraving in a bunch of words. Like you said, this is art. If someone wants a regular birdhouse that's nailed and glued together, then they can either make one or buy one. Then they can engrave it, paint it, or piss on it. Doesn't make any difference to me. But my birdhouses? No, I don't think I'd do anything to change them once they're made. That make sense? Guess you could say I'm fussy."

"I don't agree entirely, but I get it. You create the damn things and can do whatever you want with them. But what if someone decides to carve or paint one after they buy it from you or me?"

"I wouldn't give a damn at that point. If someone wants to ruin what I've created, there's nothing I can do to stop them. I'm not going to set rules or make someone sign a contract that they'll never do anything to one of these. If they're happy with what I make and pay me a fair price, that's plenty. Anything else they want to do is their choice."

"You willing to let me display it in the shop or not?"

"Sure. I'll bring it back in a day or two. But it's not for sale at any price. With our names on top, I doubt anyone would want it, but it'll be safer in your shop than me hauling it around in my saddlebags or sitting on a ledge in my rooming house. See you in a few days."

The ledge towered over a narrow canyon with a meandering creek winding its way through wildflower fields entirely absent of trees. A beautiful stairway leading from his position on the ledge all the way down to the creek was carved out of granite with incredible precision. It was wide enough for two people. Solid oak handrails lined both sides of the sturdy steps the perfect width for him. The figure of a woman suddenly appeared a few steps below him. Her head was covered by a long shawl made of intricately woven yarns. The shrill sound of a bird of prey, either a hawk or falcon, filled the air, but it was nowhere in sight. As he neared the bottom of the granite stairway, a driverless buckboard adorned in jewels and pulled by two white stallions floated down from the clouds. The woman stepped into the buckboard and vanished into a lavender colored fog that rose from the creek.

CHAPTER 21
Encounter

During the three weeks since they met, Darik and Pere had built a friendship, something neither had allowed much of over the years, not because they disliked other people *en masse* but because both were so independent. Blind trust in others who were not family members and allowing them into their personal lives was simply not how either man navigated their worlds. They engaged in conversations with others but generally avoided personal aspects of their lives, plans for the future, and any mention of Pere's late wife or especially Darik's daughter, who somehow was of interest to Pere, someone who never had children of his own.

Rebuilding the sidewalk on Pere's property took Darik a week, most of the work done in one and two-hour bursts between the time he got off work at the mill and when he had supper. He recruited another mill worker to help him for an entire Saturday for only two dollars. He thought it was a bargain, especially since the two-man effort would save him a week compared to working alone, and was pleasantly surprised when Pere paid the other man directly.

Darik's carving work on the new birdhouses was slow and steady, painfully so for Pere as the designated purchaser. Although the sidewalk was important, he was hoping for a faster turnaround since the six initial birdhouses sold within a week, all of them purchased by well-dressed women whom Pere recognized as members of Denver's self-proclaimed high society. These distinctively beautiful birdhouses had become the subject of conversations in the parlor rooms of Denver's upper echelon of wealth, and before long there was a waiting list.

As Pere had anticipated, several of his customers wanted personal inscriptions etched into their birdhouses. As a result, Darik relented from his earlier position and charged one dollar extra for the etching but kept the wording to a minimum. The etching was done as he sat propped up in bed at night.

Taking advantage of the popularity of Darik's handiwork, Pere raised the price of the birdhouses to fifteen dollars, an amount he never imagined would be met with such enthusiasm. In fact, he was surprised that demand increased after he increased the cost.

"Afternoon," the carver said to Pere as he walked into the store carrying a large cowhide knapsack over his shoulder containing several new birdhouses. "Here's the latest. Can't believe I'm making so many of these. Hell, I'm earning double on the birdhouses compared to what I earn at the mill."

"So quit your job. The mill can find someone else to do the mindless shit you're doing over there. You could set up shop as a carpenter or just have a gallery where you sell these birdhouses. I'll loan you the money to fix up a small studio if you want. None of my storefronts on this block are available, but I've got other property walking distance from here, a block east, that'd work."

"Ah, I don't know. Having a regular job is good right now. I'm trying to save enough money so I can eventually move Theresa and Lynetta from Tejada to Santa Fe. Tejada's a beautiful village, but there's nothing there for Theresa, particularly for her education. Based on what I've heard, I'm certain Lynetta will like Santa Fe, and I'll wager that she sets up another apothecary like the one she had in Castle Rock years ago. Naw, I'll keep the day job and just do the birdhouses in my spare time. Seems to be working out for both of us."

"That it is."

The door to the shop opened. Three burly men dressed in formal business attire, scraping their boots forcefully across the surface of the wooden floor, were followed by a woman with long black hair carrying an open parasol over her shoulder.

"Well, Mr. Pere, any new overpriced items you want to try and sell me today?" the largest of the men said in a thick Irish brogue unlike anything Darik had ever heard.

From the expression on Pere's face, Darik sensed his friend was not pleased to see this man, yet he was surprised when Pere replied politely in what Darik sensed was a sarcastic tone of voice. "Mr. Riley, top of the morning to you, sir, and to your associates and the lovely Sapphire who I always enjoy having stop by my establishment. I've got some new goods since your last visit. Has to be at least a month, maybe two, since you've come into my store. Make yourselves comfortable and I'll bring out something I consider to be extraordinary, perfect for a man of your taste and social status."

Never allowing his ego to get in the way of a compliment, albeit insincere, Riley nodded.

"And by the way, Mr. Riley," Pere said as his voice shifted to a sarcastic tone, "how's opium sales at your new emporium? As you know, opium's not something I'm interested in, but from one businessman to another, I'm curious if you're running the risk of saturating the marketplace by opening another den so close to the other one you've operated so successfully the last few years."

"I guess," Riley responded, glaring directly into Pere's eyes, "that the poisonous effects of the low-grade alcohol you sell at your pub is not up to the task of making my customers feel as good as they do from opium—you know, carefree and unbothered by the pressure of living in a robust city like Denver. And the good thing, at least I think it's a good thing, is that having beautiful whores available around the clock in my brothels is a great way to hedge against downturns in the local economy. We all know a man's pecker takes priority over almost everything else in life, even the pleasure of opium. Then again, smoke enough opium, as many of my clientele do, and the pecker won't work. Glad to see you've maintained your wry outlook, Mr. Pere. We're really a lot more alike than you might imagine. Nonetheless, let's see whatever it is you have in mind."

Darik was standing toward the back of the store, unable to see the faces of the two associates of Mr. Riley, men he presumed were bodyguards.

Darik could not see the woman's face from his vantage point. She wore a beautiful lace-edged white dress decorated with ornate patterns highlighted with colorful threading, sequins, and tiny pearl-like beads. The bottom of the dress dragged across the floor as she followed Riley to the largest display case.

"Mr. Riley, here you go. The finest woodworking I've ever laid my eyes on. Made by a true craftsman, an artist of the highest caliber from New Mexico who's decided to make Denver his home for the time being, and I'm the exclusive dealer for his artwork."

"I'm a cultured man, no doubt, Mr. Pere, but why in god's name would I be interested in woodworking? Any fucker can take a whittling knife and carve up a storm. Woodworking isn't what I'd call art, but as long as I'm here, let's take a look. Who knows, maybe Sapphire will find it interesting. She has a very different appreciation for this kind of thing than I do. Hell, I'm just a simple Irish businessman and she's my Chinese virgin."

Pere reached into the display case and pulled out three of Darik's finest, most detailed birdhouses.

Riley stared silently. "Well, Mr. Pere, one thing's for sure, whether I consider it artwork or handiwork, it's good. This craftsman as you call him, he knows wood. You're right. Nicest carvings I've ever seen in this cow town. Sapphire," he said in a soft voice, "what do you think? Do you consider this art? The Chinese have very different ideas about beauty and culture than the rest of us. What say you?"

Darik heard a gasp. The woman tried to smother the sound as rapidly as she uttered it. "You okay? You choking on something?" Riley asked. "Swallow something, my sweet virgin? Do you need some water?"

She turned her head from side to side and whispered softly, "No, thank you. I am fine."

"Take your time, Mr. Riley, and you too, Sapphire," Pere said, "while I bring out the most beautiful one he's created. But I'll warn you right now, it's not for sale. It's a display piece that proves he's truly a master carver."

"Better than these?" Riley asked.

"Different in some ways, but, yes, I think a little better."

Pere placed the birdhouse on a large piece of black felt atop the display case. He rotated it slowly, clockwise, until the two names, Darik and Lihua, were facing Riley and the woman.

Riley's expression suddenly changed from a curious indifference into a scowl as he grabbed the woman and jerked her forward until her forehead was pressed against the top of the birdhouse. "Nice name, Lihua, isn't it, you bitch! Want to tell me about this? What a fucking coincidence."

"Very common name for Chinese girls," the woman responded fearfully as Riley pushed her nose against the carved letters. "Many girls in China have that name. I am not the only one. Others in Denver too. Are there not more men named Riley just like you?"

A sinking feeling moved through Darik's body as he listened. A blend of dread and disbelief overtook him. He had not yet been seen by Riley nor his companions as he watched Pere's expression morph into the look of a crazed warrior preparing for battle. Pere shifted his eyes toward Darik, subtly moving his head up and to the side as if to signal him to back away. Confused initially by Pere's body language, he finally stepped further away from the group, moving next to a display rack of Stetsons at the far end of the store.

"Fucking bitch!" Riley shouted. "I don't need fucking lessons from you about anything! Of course, there's thousands of men named Riley in Ireland and America. Even a few in Denver. If it's just a goddamn coincidence we happened to walk into this goddamn place and happened to see your name next to someone named Darik, then it's just another one of the good lord's fucking miracles, isn't it!"

A toxic atmosphere filled the store as Darik listened to the bulldog-faced man continue his tirade. "Tell you what, Pere, I'll pay whatever you want for that fucking hunk of wood. Name your price. Name it. I'm a wealthy man. You know that. Money's no object."

"Like I said, the artist isn't selling this one," Pere responded abruptly. "It's a display piece on loan to me. He won't sell it. I know that for sure."

"Ask him," Riley said sternly, "and make it clear to him that anything in this town I want, I get. Tell him to pick a price and not try to fuck me. I'm a reasonable man. I want it for the mantel in my parlor. Nice way to remind this virgin bitch of her place in the whole scheme of things. Don't you think so, Mr. Pere?"

"Not sure what the point is of you coming into my store and yelling at me or at Sapphire. This is a respectable business and I'm a reasonably respectable businessman. If you'd like me to ask the artist about a selling price, I'll do it the next time he happens to come into the shop. I have no means of contacting him directly. I'll be sure to speak with him about it but in a civilized tone unlike the growling you've displayed since you entered my store."

The two men stared at one another as Pere's right hand moved under the counter where he gripped his fully loaded, ivory-handled Colt 45, a weapon he rarely fired other than for target shooting. A brawler in the local bars in his younger days in Denver, a man known for his acumen with his fists, Pere long ago outgrew hand-to-hand fighting. In the intervening years, he had earned the reputation of a marksman with pistols, a skill he displayed each July 4th at a shooting contest staged along the east side of the Platte River, a short distance from where he was now poised to protect himself, Darik, and Sapphire. No one else in the store was aware that the gun was cocked and resting in his hand.

Darik had been around enough fights at the ranch to know when a situation had gotten out of hand, that moment when logic was no longer part of the equation between two angry men. An uncharacteristic fog of violence began engulfing him as the woman said, "Riley, we need to leave. Please. Lihua is a common name. Not unusual. Many other Chinese women in Denver have the same name."

"Not that I've ever heard," Riley replied. "Not once. Fucking coincidence, my ass! What kind of virgin are you? Your name's right there in plain sight next to some piece of shit named Darik? You think I'm stupid? Didn't figure you're a lying whore like the rest of those cunts at the whorehouse. Better not be bullshitting me, you bitch," he shouted as he grabbed her by the forearm and shoved her toward the store's entrance.

Riley grabbed the woman's parasol and brought it across his knee, snapping it in two. With the same hand in which he held what was left of her parasol, he continued pushing the small woman with enough force that she stumbled, almost falling to the floor. She regained her balance, turned her head to the far corner of the store, and froze in place. Darik's eyes were glued to hers, and she wore a look of abject shock as he found himself wondering how the dead woman he once loved was standing a few feet away.

"What you starin' at fella?" one of the men accompanying Riley said in a loud, threatening tone. "This ain't your business. So look the other way, or I'll turn your head in a circle, you son of a bitch. Understand?"

Pere interrupted the man, "He's a customer. Leave him be. Don't come into my shop and threaten my customers, or you might find yourself with a large hole in center of your forehead." The pistol was now clearly visible atop the display case, resting in his right hand, now adjacent to the birdhouse. "Don't push your luck. The best thing you can do is head out of my store and regain your composure. You're bothering me like the stink of shit in a hog pen. Do I make myself clear?"

Riley glared at Pere but with hesitancy about what to do next since he had lived in Denver long enough to know the shop owner's history as a no-nonsense brawler and crack shot. "Mr. Pere, my ignorant colleague did not intend to offend or threaten your customer. I know how important customers are to businessmen like us, but pulling a gun is unnecessary. I understand this was a distasteful exhibition of my temper and ill-chosen foul language, especially within the confines of another man's place of business. Please accept my apology but also know that if you ever pull a gun on me again for whatever reason, you'd better use it. Like you, I'm also someone who doesn't appreciate being threatened. I'm sure you understand my point."

"Point taken. And from this point on, the next time you have even a small desire to enter my store, I advise you to leave your henchmen back in your velvet-lined pigsty where they can usually be found. I believe we have reached a mutual understanding on this. Yes, Mr. Riley?"

"Good day, sir," Riley replied. "I look forward to ironing out this slight misunderstanding sometime soon, possibly over drinks at your pub if that's suitable?"

"Let's give it some time, Mr. Riley. A lot of time. Time's the best way to heal things up. Don't you agree?"

Riley tipped his hat and with the other hand pushed the woman through the opened door. The two bodyguards followed without taking their eyes off Darik, who stood motionless.

Pere stared at Darik. "Hey, boy. You okay? Now that was eye-opening in addition to being life-threatening. I take it from your expression that you saw something very unsettling. Not to sound stupid, but is his Lihua the same Lihua you've told me about? Is she a ghost?"

Darik's chest heaved at a rapid pace as his breathing became impaired. He tried to speak, but no words came forth.

"Let's go to the back office and sip something strong," Pere directed his young friend. "Brandy for us both."

Darik followed him into the room behind the cash register. A blank expression on his face displaying neither anger nor joy filled the room with a level of anxiety Pere could taste.

"I take it that his Sapphire is your Lihua. You said she was dead. You said that you saw her dead as dead could be at the fire at Mrs. Brown's. What's going on?"

"No idea. I saw her burned body. Dead. I sure thought it was Lihua. No two ways about it. Not moving. Not breathing. Nothing. Burned badly. I barely recognized her, but I sure thought it was Lihua. I saw her with my own eyes. No question about it, Foster. This makes no sense."

"I'm not the smartest man in the world, not even the smartest one in Denver, that's for sure, but if that's Lihua, your Lihua, the woman Riley calls Sapphire and whom he tells everyone is a virgin, then this is a huge shit of a mess. She's always struck me like a nice girl even though I'd wondered why she'd associate with Riley. Don't know her much other than she comes into the shop—sometimes alone and sometimes with Riley and his boys. But he's not stupid, Darik, not stupid at all. She's at risk even if he believes her about the commonness of her name.

"Hell, all along I thought her given name was Sapphire," he added. "It never crossed my mind that it was a counterfeit name like the ones he gives his whores. I know he prances all around town bragging that he's got a beautiful Chinese virgin at his place. Basically brags that he owns her. I've figured he was waiting to sell her to the highest bidder, to some guy who only wants a virgin so he can be the first one to have her. Some men are into that. Me? Naw. I like the company of an experienced woman, whore or not. But this is the kind of crap that goes on in Denver that I've told you about"

"She's not a virgin," Darik replied.

"Darik, I realize that. Problem is that if Riley decides in his ignorant, uncivilized way that she's been with someone other than him and figures out that you're the guy whose already been in her knickers, he'll kill you. Won't ask you any questions. Won't want any explanations. Won't care about circumstances. You'll be dead. She'll become just another one of his whores and will become so accustomed to fucking strangers and smoking opium with his other gals that she'll basically become a dead woman. But he won't kill her. She's property. No more, no less. Can't figure out how a sweet girl like her would end up working for Riley. He's just a common criminal who's protected by the sheriff, the mayor and their people, and even someone on the governor's staff. Hell, I've heard that he has several federal marshals eating out of his hand because he gets them whores for free. They're all bought and paid for, the politicians and the others, with pussy."

"What do I do? How do I talk with her? She probably wonders why I left and never spoke with her again. She probably thinks I'm as worthless as Riley's thugs."

"No way to know if you're right, but it doesn't explain what she's doing with him. Why isn't she still at Mrs. Brown's place where you met her? Can you go talk with Mrs. Brown? I don't know the woman at all. Sounds as though she was pissed at you the day you fell out of the tree, but maybe there's a way for you to find out what's going on with Sapphire…with Lihua? You any good with a gun?"

Darik shrugged. "Average, I suppose."

"Listen, Darik, I know you're good with a knife, probably better than me, but can you protect yourself? This guy won't back off if he figures out who you are. Don't want to say you're a dead man, but there's no way local authorities will protect you or prosecute him if he harms you or Lihua."

"Spent ten years at Mulroony's ranch, Eagle Trail, and got in plenty of fights," Darik responded.

"Cowboy fights. Those are arm swinging brawls between drunk cowboys. I doubt anyone's ever been shot in a fight at the ranch. Hell no. Only in dime store novels. Might beat the shit out of another hired hand, but shoot him? No way. Knife him? Doubtful. But this wouldn't be a brawl. This would be an assassination. Only thing that would be left to do will be me getting upset about having to write a eulogy for your funeral."

Darik's mind was racing. Every detail of his encounters with Lihua five years earlier was now at the forefront of his thoughts. "Don't think Mrs. Brown will speak with me. She's got it in her head that I'm a bad guy."

"Come on, Darik! You don't really wonder if you're a good man or a bad one, do you?" Pere asked while looking into his friend's blank face.

"Average, I suppose. Done some stupid stuff. Sure. Not broken any laws and never hurt anyone intentionally. But, sure, I've made some choices that weren't all that great. A couple have bitten me in the ass."

"Thing is, Darik, Riley and others like him have a different set of rules than the rest of us. There's so much money being spread out among the sheriff's folks and the politicians that nobody's going to pay attention if you're found dead in some pile of garbage in an alley. You'll have to stay alert. You'll have to sharpen your instincts while you're here. I know you've been riding back trails for months and months avoiding mountain lions, bears, snakes, and probably some unsavory bandits without even knowing it, but here in Denver there's a different set of threats and shadows. Be careful."

Darik nodded. "You think Riley will figure this out?"

196

"He's crooked as hell, Darik, but sharp as a thorn. If he sniffs things out and learns you're the problem, he won't wait a moment to eliminate it. You."

"Not sure how I'm going to do this," Darik replied. "Better stay away from your store. But if you see Sapphire, Lihua, please let her know I didn't mean to hurt her if that's what she thinks I did. I thought she was dead, but there's no way I can talk to her. I didn't tell you this, but inside the birdhouse with our names carved on top is a note I wrote to her even though I thought she was dead and could never read it. It was just going to be my way of saying goodbye to the woman I truly loved the most. When I was trying to put it into the birdhouse a few weeks ago, that's when I fell and then got patched up at Mrs. Brown's. I wrote a new note the other day and put it inside the birdhouse before I left it here with you. It's for Lihua. Nobody else. So don't let anyone near the birdhouse. I don't want anybody to read it. I wrote it to myself since I believed I'd never see her again. I'll take the birdhouse with me when I head back to New Mexico. You can sell the rest, but that one's going with me. Maybe I'll bury it along the trail. Hell, I don't know. I really don't. It's getting time for me to head back home. I'm just not sure what to do about seeing Lihua."

"It's not uncommon for her to stroll around here on her own," Pere responded. "Not an everyday thing, mind you, but she stops in now and then by herself. Let's see what happens. If something changes I'll get word to you. I promise."

Darik nodded. "Thanks for watching my back."

The dark limestone cavern, at least twenty feet high and cold as a block of ice, was saturated with the odor of a burning log. There were no sources of light, no embers visible, yet he could see through the darkness, viewing every detail of the cavern as though it was broad daylight. He stood motionless; his boots felt bolted into the rough, rocky surface. The chill in the cavern was getting more severe by the second. Snowflakes, small ones the size of grain, began falling, sticking to the walls like flocking on Christmas trees. He heard the wooden wheels of a large wagon passing within a few feet of him. He turned in the direction of the sound expecting to see a large Conestoga wagon being pulled by several horses or oxen, but instead all he could see was a huge golden eagle resting on a limb of a cottonwood tree that suddenly appeared. The bird looked him in the eye and then flew into the darkness of the upper part of the cavern.

CHAPTER 22
Heartfelt

Pere was tending to paperwork in the back office when he heard the front door open. More than two weeks had passed since the encounter with Riley, so it took him by surprise when Lihua, the woman known as Sapphire, entered by herself.

"Mr. Pere," she said apologetically, "I am sorry Mr. Riley behaved so rudely the last time I was here."

"Are you safe? I was worried he'd hurt you. I've seen him worked up before," Pere interjected, "but never at you. Did he calm down?"

"I was not injured. He would never injure me, at least not so it would show. His anger scares me. It always has. But he believes I am worth so much that it keeps him from striking me."

"He didn't really believe your explanation about your name being carved on top of the birdhouse?"

"Confused, I believe. He now knows there are other women in Denver named Lihua, but seeing my name and Darik's on the top of the birdhouse upset him a great deal. He often behaves like a little boy having a temper tantrum. But, please, no more about Riley. How is it that Darik is in Denver? He disappeared many years ago…"

"Five is what he told me."

"He told you about us? About me? I thought I was in love with him, but he left and I never knew why. I think the word is *humiliated*. That is what I felt for so long."

"He left here the day of the fire at Mrs. Brown's, Lihua. He swore he saw you dead, burned to death. He was so heartbroken that he got on his horse, rode back to the ranch where he was working, grabbed a few things and moved away to grieve in private. His life changed that day. He was certain you had died. He returned to Denver a few weeks ago. When you walked in the store the other day and he recognized you, he thought he'd seen a ghost. He's still not sure what to think."

As Pere's explanation sank in, her eyes opened wide. "But it was not me at the fire."

"He realizes that now, but it doesn't make any sense to either of us."

Tears ran down her cheeks as she placed her hands on the top of the display case where the birdhouse rested, her birdhouse. "My sister, Daiyu, it was she who died. She was trapped on a staircase that collapsed during the fire. On the morning of the fire, she came to visit her daughter, Mei Ling. I was in the parlor when flames began in the kitchen, and I fled out the back door with Mei Ling. But Daiyu could not escape the flames. Mei Ling was only an infant, not even a year old. I had been taking care of her at Mrs. Brown's house because Daiyu worked for Riley. She lived and worked at his brothel. She did terrible things, things she despised, but did it to raise money for her daughter. But Riley kept most of it. She saved a few dollars each week and gave it to me to put away for Mei Ling. As long as she worked at Riley's brothel, he promised Mrs. Brown and Daiyu that he would leave me alone so I would not become one of his prostitutes, and he also promised he would have no contact with Daiyu's daughter, Mei Ling, who still lives at Mrs. Brown's."

"Your sister? Did Darik know you had a sister? How couldn't he have known it wasn't you? And what would Mrs. Brown have to do with someone like Riley?"

"We looked alike, much like sisters often do, but she was two years older and taller by two inches. I also think she was prettier. We had very little money when we arrived in Colorado, at least not until we met Mrs. Brown. She took us in and hired us to work in her home. Cleaning, things like that. When Daiyu got older, Mrs. Brown told us she would help her find another job. Daiyu eventually began working for Riley because it would pay more than what she could earn working for Mrs. Brown. Daiyu kept working for him, and that protected me from Riley, at least until she died. They made a deal. In trade for Daiyu working at his brothel, he let me continue to work for Mrs. Brown as long as Daiyu kept letting men pay to be with her. Riley did not want to know anything about Mei, his daughter, after she was born, so that is why I took care of her at Mrs. Brown's until the fire. My sister gave up her body and her life to keep Riley from turning me into one of his prostitutes. She was my guardian angel."

"Father? Riley's the child's father? My god, Lihua, your sister had a child by that son of a bitch? I'm sorry, my dear. Really sorry."

"Not sorry. Mei is wonderful. So smart. Beautiful. And she is safe with Mrs. Brown as long as I work for Riley. But I am not a prostitute. I am not. I am also not pure because I was with Darik. But Riley believes I am pure. I had to lie to him because he thinks I am the only Chinese woman in Denver who has not been with a man in that way. He is an evil, hateful man."

"Except Darik?"

"Yes. But no one knows anything about Darik except you and Mrs. Brown, but I never told her everything about Darik being my first and only lover. I was afraid she would be angry if she found out. Maybe she figured it out. I do not know. But if Riley finds out, he will hurt me and Mei Ling, maybe kill her. He hates her. In that way he is like many of the white people in Denver who hate the Chinese. But Riley seems afraid of Mrs. Brown, something I have never understood. She told me that as a young woman she had worked as a prostitute in a mining town before she found a husband, a man who had found gold and silver and became rich.

"She has always seemed to have a friendship or some sort of business relationship with the sheriff and the mayor, both of whom have dined at Mrs. Brown's many times at the summer house in the country by the field where I met Darik long ago and also at her home near the Capitol. I am certain that she has a great deal more money than Riley. I have heard Mrs. Brown warn him to stay away from her country home as well as from her home here in the city even though they only live a short distance apart. And she told me that she warned him to stay away from Mei Ling or she would have him shot. That is what she told me. But I do not know if she was being truthful. Something has always made me think they know each other better, more like business partners."

"She told you she warned him to stay away? Feisty woman."

"She is friends with a man who counsels the governor, an important man, and he sent someone to speak with Riley. That is what she told me. I think the other man may have threatened him in a way that Riley was not accustomed to because I have never seen him near Mei Ling. Mrs. Brown is not afraid of Riley or anyone else. Riley seems to understand how powerful Mrs. Brown is, but I have heard him say that he despises his daughter.

Mei is mixed blood, Irish and Chinese, and he does not want anyone to know. The bargain I made with him after Daiyu died is that I would take her place and stay with him but would not be a prostitute. I am a piece of fine art for him. He wants me to stay untouched by all men, a virgin; at least he thinks so. But Darik is the only man I have been with and I swear it. I thought Darik left because he hated me—maybe because I am Chinese or maybe because he had another woman and deceived me. I never knew."

Pere brought a chair over to Lihua. "Dear sweet Lihua, not hardly. I've never met such a romantic man. But his heart broke in two when he thought you'd died. He's never stopped missing you, but he has no idea it was your sister who died. He never asked anyone at Mrs. Brown's during the fire, and it's obvious that he didn't see you that day with Mei Ling. He just got on his horse and rode away after he saw the dead body. Your sister."

"As I said, Mr. Pere, I was protecting the baby, Mei Ling, when I ran to the other side of the property where we would be safe. She was so tiny. She barely knew her mother and still has no idea about Riley being her father. And she must never know. I promised Daiyu. I will lie to protect Mei and honor my sister's request. Do you understand that, Mr. Pere?"

Pere looked into her teary eyes and said, "Darik left something in the birdhouse for you. He told me that he wrote the original message a long time ago and only recently came back to Denver so he could put it in the birdhouse to honor his memory of you. But when he was climbing the tree to put the note inside, he fell and the birdhouse fell with him. I guess he must have lost that note when he hit the ground. In fact, it must have been Mei Ling who saw him fall and took him to Mrs. Brown's to get patched up."

"He saw Mei Ling? He saw Mrs. Brown?"

"Yep. Told me that the little girl is wonderful. Almost the same age as his own daughter, Theresa, maybe a little younger."

"Daughter? Darik has a child? How? Who is his wife? Was he with her when he and I…"

"No. He moved away from Denver after the fire and met up with some older gal who saved him after the lightning hit him. Truth is, I don't know all the details. That's when he met the old woman's niece, Ingrid. Young, maybe your age. They got married after a bit. But I have a hunch she knew he never stopped loving you. They had a daughter and then his wife got sick and died. Just like that, she died. Only twenty. Suddenly he was a widower with a young child. First, he lost you or thought he did—and then lost his wife. Poor boy felt as alone as someone could feel. Like most people, I've had my losses too, but it's tough to imagine how sad he must have been all these years even though he's got a daughter he loves."

"Where is she? His daughter? Is she here?"

"No, she's in some little village in New Mexico. She lives with Darik's friend who's like a grandmother to the girl. Sounds like the old lady made Darik leave New Mexico after his wife died so he could sort himself out a little and be a better father to Theresa. This gal didn't want his sadness to ruin the little girl's life."

"This is not fair to him," Lihua responded. "This changes so much. I was never angry with him. I just never understood why he vanished. I thought something about me was wrong and that he hated me."

"Not at all, Lihua. Not at all," Pere replied.

"Mrs. Brown said she will take care of Mei Ling until my niece is older and finds a nice Chinese man to marry," she continued. "It could be ten years, maybe more, so I must stay with Riley. I hate him. I hate being away from my niece, but I promised my sister I would always protect Mei Ling, and the only way this can happen is for me to be with Riley. I have no choice."

Pere took the birdhouse from the display case and set it on top of a large piece of felt. Lihua stroked it a few times as though it was an old friend, leaned over, and then gave it a gentle kiss. She reached into the opening and wiggled her fingers around until she found Darik's note:

Lihua, I will never let go of
your spirit. Darik

Her tears dripped onto the top of the case, several drops onto the note. She cupped her face and sobbed. Every thought she had about Darik's disappearance dissolved in an instant, a series of presumptions she created and had convinced herself about for five years as her own broken heart failed to heal.

"Riley will kill Darik. I know he will," she said.

"That's what I told him. Darik's tough, but Riley isn't the kind of man Darik's used to being around. He doesn't realize, not fully, that Riley's a rattlesnake; least he didn't until I explained things to him the day he saw you here."

"Do you see him often? Is there a way you can give him a message? I want to speak with him. I need to apologize."

"No, Lihua, you don't need to apologize. And neither does he. You two just made decisions based on bad information, maybe no information. We all do it. Riley did it the other day. Well, I guess his presumption ended up being mostly correct about you and Darik. I've done it myself—made bad decisions on the spur of the moment—maybe because it kept me from having to deal with distasteful situations with people I didn't want to be near. Hell, I don't know why. I still have a bad habit of making up terrible stories in my mind, personal myths you could say, and then believe the lies I've created to protect myself. Sometimes it cuts me off from everyone. It's a bad habit, but it distances me from pain; at least I always thought it did. But not any longer."

"I will write a note and leave it for Darik," she said.

"Put it in your birdhouse. I won't let anyone near it. But you've got to be careful, Lihua. Really careful. Riley's got people scattered all over this part of town doing his bidding, doing his spying. Did you make sure you weren't followed?"

"I never checked, Mr. Pere. I go on walks by myself all the time."

"Things have changed. Maybe you need to create a distraction to confuse Riley and his thugs? We need to make your visits to my store look like they have another purpose than just chatting. Pick out a gift for Riley that he'll think's an apology from you. Make that snake feel special. It'll be my treat. He already thinks the world revolves around him, so getting him a gift might work."

She smiled, placed her hand atop his and said, "A walking cane. He does not need one, but when he sees a rich white man walking down the street with a beautiful cane, I see his eyes light up. He would never buy one for himself. He would not. Please let me see a cane."

"Good idea. They're over by the hat racks. I've got a special one in mind, a beautiful hand-carved one from Mexico. He'll look perfect with this cane."

He pulled out the cane, dark wood, nearly black, with small, intricate pieces of embedded turquoise, quartz, and red coral that formed the shape of a pair of small diamonds.

"Oh, it is beautiful but must cost too much. I do not want you to give me something so expensive."

"Don't worry," Pere replied. "Darik's birdhouses are selling fast and these canes rarely get bought. This'll be a good way to reduce my inventory. Please, no arguing. I'll wrap it up and you can take it to Riley."

"You do not need to do this, but in my culture it is impolite to argue about a gift or kind gesture. I am indebted. Thank you, Mr. Pere."

"You're welcome. Now write your note and put it inside the birdhouse," he added, "while I wrap up the cane. Darik'll come by the shop in a few days with more birdhouses. Nothing firm on the schedule—just a hunch now that he's seen you again. One way or the other, he'll be here in a few days."

* * *

Nearly a week had passed since Lihua placed her note inside the birdhouse. Darik had kept a low profile by staying in his boarding house when he was not at the mill. Pere, concerned about maintaining secrecy, had not tried to reach the young man. Finally, out of a sense of desperation, he paid the stable boy at the nearby carriage works to take a sealed note to Darik advising him to stop by the store as soon as possible. The boy often ran small errands for Pere, so nothing about this task would seem unusual.

Late that same afternoon, an hour before sundown, Darik entered the store through the back door carrying a large cowhide bag containing several new birdhouses. "Pere! I've got a delivery."

"It's about time. I'm down to one birdhouse. I knew once one of those society ladies made a purchase, the others would follow suit," Pere replied.

"I'm busy at the mill. Only able to carve in my spare time, and there isn't much of that. So why'd you really want me to come down here so urgently? Your note confused me."

Pere reached down into the large display case and lifted the special birdhouse. "Something inside for you."

Darik's puzzled expression was replaced by a smile as he removed the folded paper:

> *Darik, I know the truth. I am sorry we lost*
> *so much time living in sadness. I am not*
> *sad any longer. I am a blossoming sunflower.*
> *I love you.   Lihua*

Darik collapsed on the nearest chair, his head shaking in disbelief, yet a sense of calm, something he had not experienced in years, began flowing through his body. "When was she here?"

"A week ago. I warned her to be careful. Same for you. Riley's people are all around this part of town, even more than usual. You two are at risk if someone figures out you're the one making the birdhouses and that it's your name on the birdhouse. Just make sure you bring me a lot of inventory before Riley shoots you," Pere pleaded sarcastically.

"Did he hurt her? Is she safe? How do I get a message to her?"

"Your birdhouse. It's the only safe way. She'll come back in a day or two. You two can exchange notes until you figure out what to do. But I'm warning you again, Riley's no fool. If he figures this out, you won't live long enough to see Lihua again."

"I get it, Pere. Please let me have paper and pen. I want to meet her someplace safe. Maybe here in the store? Is it safe here?"

"No, not safe at all. If you're going to do this, you need to pick several locations, maybe along the river or by the large gazebo in the park by the new cemetery, someplace where you can take a casual walk and meet up. But it can't be long. It's got to look normal. Can't be suspicious. Someone'll notice if there's a pattern of you two meeting up. You'll have to meet in different places and then hope nobody will care much about a white man spending even a little time with a Chinese woman in public."

While Darik knew the advice from Pere was accurate, he conveyed a look of disbelief.

"Trust me," Pere added, "down deep he's a wild son of a bitch. You saw that when he was in the store. Jealousy isn't something to ignore with someone like Riley. Don't push things. Be patient."

Darik finished writing his message, folded the paper, and put it inside the birdhouse. Pere then placed the birdhouse back on the upper shelf of the display case and locked the cabinet door.

"Just let me know how I can help. Anything. I know you don't carry a pistol, but you're still carrying that hunting knife in your sheath, aren't you?"

Darik answered confidently, "Right here. Sharper than a razor and I know how to use it."

CHAPTER 23
Recapture

Lihua stopped by Pere's store three days later, Darik a day later, and Lihua again two days after that to exchange notes.

A pervasive fear had been running through her since she left her first note along with an intense joy that began when she and Darik first made eye contact at the store. The turn of events seemed like a fairy tale, yet she knew it was important to avoid expectations that had the potential to result in another broken heart.

The mood in Riley's home had changed dramatically since he saw the birdhouse bearing Lihua's name. The brusque and violent tone he displayed towards her that day, something he previously reserved for the other Chinese women who worked for him, had become commonplace. An ever present tension now filled the air. Absent was the boyish verbal fawning over Sapphire that he formerly displayed.

After exchanging notes for two weeks, today, Sunday, was the day Darik and Lihua agreed to meet in person for the first time. Their rendezvous point would be the bandstand in the small park located walking distance from the new capitol building, more than a mile from Riley's corrupt businesses and nearly a mile from his spacious home located a short distance from Mrs. Brown's primary dwelling.

Lihua's plan was to initially head in the opposite direction from the park for a few minutes, meandering back toward downtown to avoid undue attention, then hire a horse-drawn cab to take her within walking distance of the park, and then complete the remaining distance on foot.

She was nervous, continually glancing over her shoulder until she finally flagged down a cab. Once she boarded and gave directions to the driver, a disheveled looking man who was silent during the first half of the ride, she felt safer.

As they approached the park, the driver said, "You're far from your neck of the woods for a Chinese, ain't you? No law against Chinese being up here in Capitol Hill, but people living by the park ain't used to seeing a fashionable Chinese woman unless she's walking to or from a housekeeping job. The only Chinese as pretty as you that these people know about are working in the whorehouses. What's your story? You can't have friends living up here. Looking for someone to keep you company this afternoon? I know who you are; you're Riley's virgin. I'd like to be the first man to fuck you. I got time and money."

Surprised by his crude comments, she glared before taking a silver dollar from her handbag and tossing it to him, making sure it landed on the ground so he would have to step down from the buggy to retrieve it.

"I am certain Mr. Riley would be interested to know what you have suggested. Would you prefer I tell him, or would you rather drive to his office and discuss it in person?"

"Fucking slant-eyed whore. Nobody, even Riley, would believe you. I'm not afraid of Riley or anyone else. You're just a whore dressed up like one of these high society bitches."

She had not thought about being recognized in this neighborhood, having convinced herself that anyone who might have followed her would have given up by now. The driver's comments took her off stride. Not only was she unaccustomed to feeling so vulnerable, but she had been verbally accosted for being Chinese and was now relying on her intuition to diffuse the situation.

"Did that dollar cover the ride?" she inquired.

"Half-dollar would have done."

"Keep the change. Maybe you will find someone else to offend. I have not yet decided if I will report you to Riley."

He snapped the buggy whip, jerked the reins to the right, and began heading away. Lihua watched until the cab was out of sight and then walked toward the elevated bandstand in the center of the half-acre park. She scanned the area, noticing two uniformed constables approaching from the north. Both stared at her disapprovingly, a typical reaction she and all other Chinese residents of Denver had come to expect. She avoided making direct eye contact, spun her parasol slowly as its shaft rested on her shoulder, and maintained a slow and steady stride.

To her left, to the east of the bandstand, Darik had tied off his horse and was walking around the large wooden structure in a counterclockwise direction.

In a matter of seconds, they made eye contact and exchanged smiles as they passed by one another slowly enough to exchange brief whispered greetings, but then continued walking while also scouring the area to see if anyone was paying attention to them.

He spoke louder when they passed one another on the next revolution around the bandstand and came to a near stop. "You look beautiful, Lihua, even more than I remembered. I'm so sorry. I wish things had been different."

She smiled as tears formed in her eyes as they slowly passed one another. "We both have been living our lives. It is fine, Darik. We will make up for the lost time," she said as her voice became inaudible.

Darik stopped walking, sat down on a park bench, and scanned the park grounds in order to look for Riley or his people as well as to alter the pattern he and Lihua established on their initial trips around the bandstand.

"You are so handsome, Darik," she whispered as she walked past him several minutes later. "I missed you. Every day I have missed you."

Lihua stopped and sat down on a bench on the far side of the bandstand, no more than fifty feet from Darik. They made eye contact and the reassuring glances they exchanged signified that their powerful connection still existed. While she remained seated, Darik stood up and meandered around to the back side of the bandstand, walking past her much more slowly than before.

"I want to kiss you. I want to hold you," he said as though he were demanding rather than asking.

His heart pounded. Sensations similar to what he experienced when they made love five years earlier raced through him, and he nearly reached out to grab her hand as they passed by one another a second time. Instead, to his surprise, she reached out and tapped his hand with hers. He felt as though all his dreams had finally come true.

Darik stopped in midstride, turned his head back toward her while waving in a subtle manner, and walked to his horse. Lihua stood, turned to the north, back towards where the buggy had dropped her off earlier, and began walking in the direction of Riley's home, a thirty minute walk at this pace.

Every other day for the next two weeks they met in various locations including Union Station, the grounds of the new state capitol building, and other shops located far from Riley's businesses.

Pere did not question either one of them about their unusual situation when they stopped by his store to leave new messages, and he only provided commentary when one or the other asked for specific advice. Although he was eight years older than Darik, by default he found himself taking on a fatherly role that allowed him to apply his natural pragmatism to make sure the two of them remained safe.

Despite taking precautions to protect Darik and Lihua when they were near the store, Pere was certain that Riley's men were stationed in strategic locations where they could follow Lihua's movements, and he suggested several additional places where they would have privacy and some degree of safety.

* * *

"Lihua," Pere said as she entered the store displaying a cautious expression, "Why the sad face?"

"Your warnings are correct," she answered. "It feels like Riley's people are watching me all the time no matter where I go. Maybe I am imagining it. I am worried that Darik will be hurt."

"Like I've said a dozen times, there's almost no other Chinese women, beautiful or not, walking around alone in the white neighborhoods. In fact, it's pretty rare to see even in this part of town. Keep your voices low. Use your eyes. Don't make yourselves obvious."

"You are correct. I know you are. But it is so difficult because we want to be together. I do not know if I have the patience to do this."

"What's your option? Either you pace yourself or you'll never get the chance to be with one another. Your time will come, just not yet."

Lihua placed her hand on Pere's. "You are the big brother I had always imagined. Someday I will thank you in a more meaningful way."

He smiled as he felt small tears forming that he did not want her to see. "Never had children of my own, but I'm lucky to have a brother with a wife and family. My wife's been dead for years, but I knew on the day I buried her that I'd never settle for someone else who didn't measure up. So I'm telling you to be more patient than you think's possible. Whatever your destiny is intended to be will reveal itself sooner or later. That's just how things work out."

Soft hands were stroking Lihua's legs lightly, making her feel as though she were covered in the finest silk as she lay prone upon a billowy cloud hovering over a massive wildflower field. Her eyes were closed, clenched tightly, yet she could see a vividly colored rainbow flickering like holiday candles. Lips brushed across her lips, her tongue tasting flavors of bliss that she recognized to be Darik's despite not being with him in many years. She realized she was dreaming, but her lucid awareness caused her to drift in and out as though she could actually direct the content of the dream. The sounds of morning were highlighted by a rooster crowing in the distance as the hands and kisses vanished.

CHAPTER 24
Outrage

Riley was known to be dictatorial in his communications with employees and had a reputation for physically abusing them, often knocking them to the ground or using other forms of intimidation to force them into doing their jobs.

Following the discovery of the birdhouse at Pere's store, he had become obsessed with an invisible man named Darik whom he was convinced was involved with Lihua, his Sapphire.

"Fucking cunt!" he shouted at O'Connor, his senior bodyguard. "That Chinese bitch must think I'm a goddamn fool not to know something's going on. If I find the son of a bitch who's been fucking her, he'll regret ever being born, and she'll have a price to pay that'll spin her in circles."

"I haven't seen her with anyone at all, Mr. Riley. Honest, I even…"

"Shut your goddamn mouth. No more excuses. I know what I know. You're a fucking stupid excuse for a man, O'Connor. Get out of my sight. Do a better job or find a new one. I'll bet a hundred dollars she's been meeting with him right in front of your eyes. Pere's behind this. I know how he operates. He's playing me for a fucking fool."

O'Connor avoided making direct eye contact with Riley. "I've had my best people follow Pere no matter where he's gone—his shop, the bank, his brother's place—everywhere. Even got a friend at Pinkerton who owed me a favor to help out. Me and my boys have seen the bitch go into Pere's store a few times, always by herself, and even had someone follow her in but haven't seen her talk with anyone but Pere."

"Bullshit."

"Honest, Mr. Riley. She looks at that birdhouse each time she's in the store, really close up, and one of the boys thought he'd seen her put something inside it when he was standing by the front window. But Pere put the goddamn thing back into that display case before he could check it out."

"What the hell? One of your fucking idiots saw her put something in the birdhouse, and you didn't tell me until now? You fucking fool! How can you be so stupid? That Chinese cunt's leaving messages for the bastard who's getting in her knickers. He's probably doing the same thing, leaving messages. But since you haven't figured out what the bastard looks like, this son of a bitch just keeps pissing in your face. I'm sure Pere organized this. Get over to his store and bring me whatever's in that birdhouse, and do it now. Don't let him put that piece of wooden crap away without you seeing what's inside. Hell, since you still can't read a fucking word of English, just bring it to me. If you have to strong arm Pere to get into the birdhouse, then do it. Just watch out for that fancy Colt he keeps under the counter. Don't trust any of your fucking idiots for this job. You take care of this yourself! Understand me! Do you understand me?"

"Mr. Riley, there's no way he'll let me or anyone else near it. He's got no problem pulling that gun on me or anyone else including you."

"You're afraid of him? Fucking afraid of a storekeeper? That's what you're telling me? Jesus Christ, get out of my fucking sight! In fact, stay away from Pere's store. Don't get near it! I don't need you fucking this up worse. I'll handle this myself."

O'Connor, hat in hand, stepped back from Riley's desk, reached for the door handle and was about to leave when a paper weight struck him in the back of the head with such force that his forehead smashed into the beveled glass section of the door, shattering it into dozens of small pieces. Blood flowed from his forehead.

"And don't you fucking dare bleed on my floor, you piece of shit! Get someone to clean up this mess."

O'Connor, dazed by the assault, regained his composure as blood oozed down his face and onto his shirt. "Yes, sir, Mr. Riley. Right away."

CHAPTER 25
Foreboding

Darik rode his ten-year-old palomino to the northwest entrance of the city cemetery, the location where he and Lihua planned on meeting, arriving thirty minutes before her. He dismounted, led the horse around the perimeter fence counterclockwise, and scanned the grounds to make sure he had not been followed.

A funeral was underway. He watched as four pall bearers a hundred feet away, large men wearing some sort of dark uniforms, lowered a light colored casket into the grave. Only a handful of people were in attendance, the largest of whom was a man wearing the silver shield of a marshal, a man Darik had seen roaming around near Pere's shop a few times. Darik figured it was a coincidence that he would see the same man at the cemetery but kept moving and tried to appear unconcerned.

However, at that precise moment, the man looked up and nodded as though he recognized him. Darik was surprised by the man's glance but raised his eyebrows and tapped the front brim of his cowboy hat. The man did not make further eye contact and turned his attention to the funeral.

Darik continued walking toward the southeast corner of the cemetery which was absent of activity other than a few magpies. Once he had moved a reasonable distance from the funeral, he tied his horse to a fence post and walked along the northern fence line. He saw a woman approaching with a parasol resting on her right shoulder, but he did not change the length or speed of his stride even as his heart began pounding as though it would explode.

"You look beautiful," he said to Lihua as their pace slowed to a near stop. "Do you think it's safe for us to talk here?"

"I am not sure. Only a few people at a funeral are in the cemetery, so I think it might be safe for a moment or two. But not longer. Mr. Pere keeps warning me about being seen with you."

"Me too. He acts like we're children. He worries like a big brother. But I know he wants us to be together, not dead. His fretting about Riley is real, so we just gotta be careful."

"I have always wondered how Riley knows so much about what takes place in Denver. He seems to know everyone, even those who do not visit his businesses."

"He keeps his ear close to the ground, that's for sure," Darik replied.

"I do not understand. Why is his ear down there?"

Darik sighed. "Just an old saying from trail hands. Pretty sure they learned it from the Indians. It means that someone has a lot of skill in watching out for things others might not be aware of, and that's important when you're out on the trail somewhere. Lots safer."

"Did you have your ear to the ground when the lightning struck you?" she asked in a coy tone.

"No," he answered, "I wasn't paying attention to anything because I was daydreaming about you right when the lightning blew everything into thousands of pieces."

She smiled and began walking past him at a slow pace, her lips puckered just enough to blow him a kiss. "I want to walk around one more time, but only a short distance, and then we can turn around and chat some more. Is that safe?"

"I think so. Sure. But I wanted to tell you that your English is really good. You've learned a lot over the years. You speak it better than me."

"I have been taking English classes for several years. I feel so much better being able to speak English this well. I especially love writing and reading poetry. I sometimes understand the poems but not always."

"Never read a poem in my life.'

"Do you read English?"

"Not too bad. Not fancy stuff. Mulroony, my boss at the ranch, made sure to teach me enough to get by. I can read bills of sale and shopping lists, things like that, so sure, I read and write good enough to not feel like a fool."

"I can teach you more English," she said as the distance between them widened, "if we can ever get some privacy. Would you like that?"

Darik smiled. "Yes."

Several minutes passed before they had each turned around and began walking back toward one another.

"Nobody's left in the cemetery," he said as they walked within a few feet of one another. He leaned forward, placed both hands on her cheeks, and brought her lips to his, an electrifying kiss that had been delayed for five years. Darik felt as though he been transported into another dimension as his eyes remained wide open during the embrace, wide enough to scan the area around them to make sure they were alone.

"Never did I think we would kiss again," she said in a blissful tone. "Never. I dreamt about it. I hoped. But I had given up and no longer believed we would ever see one another again. You became a dream for me, a fantasy."

"Don't really know what dreams are made of," he replied, "but I never stopped dreaming—always remembered how you felt against my body, how you tasted, and how you smelled. I sometimes worried that I had forgotten the details of what you actually looked like, but I always kept a picture of you in my heart. I can't explain it. For a long time, I wondered if it had all been a dream. I wasn't sure, not at all. But I never forgot what I felt the day we met in the sunflower field. I wondered if we were meant to be together forever. I never imagined we'd have this strange journey. Together and then apart and then together again. Maybe it was all meant to happen like this so we'd love each other even more."

"Destiny. That is the word I was taught to describe the way certain things, important things in our lives, are meant to occur," she said. "I have noticed that for many of those people who go to church on Sundays, this destiny might be called God's will. But I do not go to those churches, so I think of it as the natural order of things. My grandmother used to call it the connection between what we call the living and what we call the dead, what we call alive like people, animals and plants and what we call not alive like rocks and sand. Like my grandmother, I believe all things, everything, has a life of its own, an energy that connects everything together whether or not we think it is alive or not. She believed this and so do I. How is that different from what you learned in the forests where you grew up with your grandparents and what you know about the wood from the trees you carve? They are alive and they have some sort of soul or energy or purpose. Even your carving tools have this energy. I felt the power of the first birdhouse you gave me. That one and all the others you have carved are alive. I believe that. Do you?"

Darik hesitated as her words soaked in. "I've always believed that trees speak to me in some sort of a magical language that only I understand. I believed, especially when I was a little boy, that my grandfather had taught me to speak with trees. But I've learned that this connection is between all things, those breathing things and those not breathing. Yes, it's real.

"The ledge in Sedona where I spent a night of living dreams that can't be explained in normal ways, the journey I took in my mind, or maybe out of it—that night proved that it isn't only trees that I can speak with but that, if I get quiet enough and listen carefully enough, I can understand more about our world than I ever thought possible. My friend in Sedona is a wise man in his tribe. He speaks with the rocks, the cliffs, the canyons, the sand, the cactus, trees and flowers, all the animals, and the sky itself. I saw it and I was part of it too, but it made no sense until I actually heard the conversations he was having with nature. And Lynetta, my friend who's taking care of my daughter, she also speaks with everything in nature. She listens, she watches, and she seems connected to everything. It's not like either one of them is a god. It's more like they both see a bigger plan for life. Maybe it's what you called destiny."

Their lips never parted as they whispered, his hands resting on her hips and pulling her into him so tightly that he could feel her body pulsating.

"We must stop," she cautioned. "I must return to Riley's home. I do not want him to be suspicious."

"Whoever's been teaching you English must be great. You speak it so much better than I do. Who's your teacher?"

"You will laugh," she replied, "because my teacher is the wife of Foster Pere's younger brother, Nathan. Nathan is a deputy marshal and he is a wonderful man. His wife is an angel."

"His brother's a marshal? Wonder why he's never mentioned it?

"Foster and Nathan are brothers from different mothers. Nathan's wife told me that Foster's mother died shortly after he was born. His father raised him for several years, I think until Foster was ten. His father married a mixed blooded woman, the daughter of a slave with a white father and black mother. Then she gave birth to Nathan. He is a very tall man, taller than Foster, and is just as considerate. They are so much alike. People say he and his big brother are the most honest men in Denver. I believe that. From what I have learned from his wife, Nathan answers to no one but himself and to her, of course, and to Foster who is more like a father to him than an older brother."

"I thought Riley owned all the police and politicians?"

"He has tried. But not everyone here is dishonest. I do not know the names of everyone Riley controls. I have seen many of them at Riley's home and at his businesses. He is very private and I am not always brought along. I also do not know who controls Riley, but I do not believe he is the actual boss. Something tells me that he is the most visible person but that he is someone's employee, someone with greater power and influence in Denver. I am almost certain he takes orders from someone else if that makes sense."

"Seriously? What does Pere think? He knows a lot about what goes on in Denver, but he's never said anything about it."

"I do not know. But I believe there is a group of people, a small, secret group, some of whom are in government, also some bankers and some criminals like Riley, but I think he is just one of the lesser bosses, not the real boss."

They exchanged another long and endearing smile as their conversation ended. Darik began walking towards his horse and was pleased that when he turned around, Lihua was standing motionless and watching him. She waved, turned, and slowly resumed her meandering walk to Riley's sprawling home in Capitol Hill.

Thoughts of the grandmother she left in China years earlier and the advice the wise woman had shared back then washed over her. During the recent weeks since she saw Darik after his five-year absence, she admitted to herself that the stories she had concocted about his unexplained disappearance were mere presumptions. They were nothing more than nightmares, dark myths she created. Some of them she now realized were due to being young and unaccustomed to the mysteries of the American culture. But now, finally, the idea of discovering happiness with Darik seemed plausible.

The acerbic, angry sound of a man's voice took her by surprise as she daydreamed. "Sapphire, you fucking bitch! You fucking Chinese whore! Who the fuck's that man? Is he the son of a bitch I've been looking for?"

Startled, she turned as Riley, atop his mahogany-colored Morgan, Diablesa, pulled up alongside. "Just a man who was walking. A stranger."

"And the kiss? That was for a fucking stranger? You're nothing more than a whore just like the rest of them, a fucking cunt who can be bought and sold just like your fucking dead sister."

Riley jerked the reins, abruptly yanking the horse into Lihua, forcefully knocking her to the ground. She looked up at her assailant and the statuesque mare.

Petrified at her vulnerable position beneath what would be the next stride of the horse, tears streamed down her cheeks as the shaking of her body generated so much fear that she became paralyzed. Riley had trapped her. Thoughts of her grandmother and of a lifetime with Darik fled from her and were replaced by a flood of panic.

The horse stared into her eyes, seemingly cognizant of Lihua's fear, yet despite Riley's repeated attempts to get the horse to step on the woman, Diablesa refused his loud commands that were accompanied by the use of the whip and repeated kicks into its flanks. "Fucking horse! Diablesa! Goddamn you! Kill that bitch! Stomp that whore!"

Lihua had resigned herself to the helplessness of the situation. *At least* she thought, *we were able to kiss one another again.*

Enraged, Riley dismounted while still holding a thin, black-handled whip in his right hand. He lifted it into the air, held it stationery for a moment, and then brought it down violently on Lihua's shoulder with enough force to slice her sleeve into two pieces, but she was not cut despite the sharp pain in her shoulder. She remained silent, fearful that anything she might say would cause even more aggression. She watched in terror as he remounted the horse.

"Cunt! Fucking cunt! You bitches are all alike! Nothing about you is appealing to me—not even your cunt—except that you're going to start spreading your legs to make me a lot of money if I don't kill you right now! Trust me, you little whore, the white men who paid to fuck your sister day after day, just like they still do to all the other Chinese women who work for me, do it in secret only because their own wives fuck like missionaries. Those prissy women aren't any good at pretending to enjoy being fucked, so they pretend to ignore the fact that I provide their husbands with women who know how to pleasure a man.

That's what keeps their damn marriages together. But unlike the whores who work for me, those so-called respectable white women in Capitol Hill, Mrs. Brown's guests during afternoon tea, don't spread their legs for just any son of a bitch cowboy with a few dollars in his pocket. Your dead sister, that bitch, she didn't waste herself on those cheap ass cowboys. Nope, she only fucked the wealthiest, most powerful men around here—the mayor, the governor, and, hell, she even fucked a senator. See, these white society women are just high class whores who try to ignore the fact that my Chinese whores are sucking their husbands' cocks. These lifeless white women only do what's required with the rich white men they marry to live a life of luxury compared to Chinese trash like you. Problem with your sister is she liked fucking so much that she didn't care whose cock was inside her. How about you?"

In his rage, he failed to notice the sound of a horse galloping towards him. With pistol in hand, cocked and ready to fire, Foster Pere brought his horse to a sudden stop next to Diablesa. Riley was stunned by the changing circumstances as Pere shouted, "Riley, you're a prick! A goddamn prick!" He placed the white-handled revolver against the side of Riley's head. "Drop the fucking whip and back up as carefully as you can. I don't need an excuse to blow your fucking head off."

Riley's eyes shifted to the left although his head remained in place. "Not a smart move, Pere. This'll get you killed. But you already know that. Holster the gun or I'll let Diablesa crush the cunt's fucking chest flat as a board. Only thing left of her will be a pile of fabric."

"One! Two! Three!" Pere began shouting with a certainty that caught Lihua off guard as she remained frozen in place. "Your fucking choice, Riley, you bastard!"

A shot rang out. Lihua gasped as Riley fell from the horse and rolled on the ground. But there was no blood and no obvious wound, simply Riley shouting. "Dead man! You miserable son of a bitch! Fucking fired that gun next to my ear! I can't hear a goddamn thing, you bastard! I'll kill you!"

She watched Pere, a man whom she had never seen express anything other than a calm and gentle demeanor until the day she and Riley walked into the store and saw the birdhouses, re-cock the pistol and fire two shots a few feet to the side of Riley. Frightened by the gunfire, the horse backed away from Lihua and galloped away at full speed, leaving Riley without a means of escape.

"Lihua, please gather yourself and move away," Pere commanded. The single undamaged strap over her left shoulder remained intact as she rose. She stepped back one stride, smiled at Pere, and then uncharacteristically stepped forward and kicked Riley, still laying on the ground, in the side of his leg.

"Chinese bitch!" he screamed as his mature Irish brogue was replaced by the voice of a child throwing a fit. "You'll join this bastard in hell! You will! I promise!"

Pere dismounted, placed the revolver back in his holster, and handed the reins to Lihua and pointed to the fence line. "Here you go, Lihua. Why don't you walk Ajax a little ways from here, maybe over by that scrub oak? I'll be with you shortly."

She led the animal away without turning her head to see what he would do next. "I will wait for you over there," she replied.

Pere extended his hand to Riley to help him to his feet, but the furious man pushed it away, sprang to his feet and dove headlong into Pere's thighs, knocking him to the ground. Pere rolled to the side, rose to one knee, and charged into Riley, knocking him back to the ground. He began pummeling the man's face. His knuckles became bloodied from the blows to Riley's head, but he was oblivious to everything. Each time Riley attempted to counter, Pere struck him again although the next series of blows were to Riley's midsection. Riley was gasping, unable to breathe, praying in his own demented silence for a divine spirit to intervene.

Blood poured from Riley's mouth and nose. His white linen shirt was splattered in red, his tie dangling, and the knees of his pants were in shreds.

"You have a choice, Riley. You can either stand up and begin walking home, and maybe you'll find your horse; maybe you won't, or you can stay here and I'll beat you to death. You decide. Nobody, not a solitary soul in Denver will really care if you're dead, not even the politicians and police, and certainly not the people who work for you or whomever controls you like a puppet. Nobody'll miss you. Someone else will replace you, and it won't take long—someone who might even be a worse human, though I don't think it's possible. What I suggest, strongly suggest, is that you begin walking. You already know I'd just as soon kill you right here and now, but I don't want any witnesses around when I finally do it. Not fair to my friend, Lihua, to ask her to testify in court about what she might see me do next. And while almost nobody else but me will care that you tried to kill a Chinese woman, nobody would ever believe that a shopkeeper like me beat your ass to death. At worst, it'll be considered self-defense. Maybe even heroic. Once you're gone, you're gone."

Riley slowly came to his feet, began walking away, and then turned slightly to his left. As he did, his right hand, which was out of sight from Pere, withdrew a small pistol from his boot top, a derringer, that he fired without warning, the bullet glancing across the taller man's shoulder. Without any hesitation, Pere pulled the white-handled pistol from his holster and shot Riley just above the knee on the outside portion of the leg. Riley screamed, dropped the derringer, and began cursing.

Pere pulled a large handkerchief from his pocket and tossed it to the wounded man. "Tie off that wound or you'll to bleed to death right here in the new cemetery. That would be fitting, wouldn't it?! Don't bother returning it. Keep it as a reminder. And if I find out you've touched anyone else who works for you, I'll shoot you right between your fucking eyes. If I'd wanted to kill you now, you'd be on your way to Hell. Looks like the bullet passed through your leg, but I'm guessing the blood loss could be substantial, maybe fatal, so I advise you to take care of yourself."

Riley remained silent as he tied a makeshift tourniquet around his throbbing leg. Once the tourniquet was in place, he began struggling back toward his nearby home in Capitol Hill, walking with an obvious limp.

Pere walked over to Lihua, still holding the reins to his horse. "You are injured. Let me fix it. Please," she said.

"Just a scratch, young lady. Damn careless of me. Never should have let the son of a bitch turn to the side and get the drop on me. Nathan won't let me hear the end of it. I could have gotten us both killed. I'll be fine. There's some whiskey and cotton cloth in the saddlebag. Could you grab them for me? Are you all right, Lihua? Did he hurt you?"

"I am fine. I do not know how to thank you. You saved me. He would have let the horse kill me."

"Naw," he replied, "that's a smart horse. She wasn't about to step on your pretty face. I suspect the horse is long gone, and Riley won't ever see her again. Her name, Diablesa, it means 'she-devil' in Spanish," he said with a laugh. "He might have thought his horse was a she-devil, but I watched the horse refuse to move towards you. I think that horse is actually an angel sent here to protect you, kind of like the warrior horse, Pegasus. Have you heard of this mythological creature?"

Lihua shook her head, "No. Still learning English from Nathan's wife and am sorry I never told you that I know her. But, no, I have not read about Pegasus. I will ask her about it at the next class," she replied, seemingly oblivious of the depth of this crisis.

Pere sighed as he poured whiskey on his wound and dabbed the blood with the cloth. "My sweet young Lihua, there won't be a next class. I'm going to make a suggestion, in fact, more than a suggestion. You don't have to abide by it, but, trust me, I'm going to make the same one to Darik. You two need to leave Denver immediately if you have any hope of spending your lives together. You can stay overnight at my store. I'll send someone to the mill to get Darik. Tomorrow, at sunrise, you two are going to take one of my small, covered buckboards to wherever you need to go to be safe, maybe to Darik's place in New Mexico. That's far enough away that Riley won't bother you anymore. He still doesn't know much about Darik other than what he looks like from a distance. You need to leave Denver. Call it a wedding present, the buckboard, but you have to go and not return. You both need a fresh start. If Riley doesn't bleed to death while he's walking back to his home, I'm sure he'll muster his crew and come looking for you, Darik, and me. You need to get some distance from Riley."

She stared in silence.

"I'm not trying to scare you, Lihua. Well, hell, sure I am. This is the real thing. Riley's a poor excuse for a man, a truly bad man. I got the drop on him and took him by surprise when I rode up, but the only reason I came out here to the cemetery to find you is because Nathan attended a funeral and saw Darik moseying around the fence line. Figured he was waiting for you. My brother rode back to the store and told me you two were out here together. But he'd already seen one of Riley's people watching the cemetery, the guy with the buggy who brought you out here once before. Riley owns them all. He found out you've been coming here from that driver, a lowlife who wanted reward money. Nathan's been keeping an eye on Darik the past few weeks. But just as I figured, Riley's folks have kept track of everywhere you've gone, hoping to see you and Darik together. Listen, the important people in this city, the ones my brother and I trust the most, are tired of Riley and the corruption he and others have woven into our city. Denver's growing up, slow at times, but growing up. Time for bandits like Riley to be gone."

"Darik will not leave without first going after Riley," she said.

"He won't have the chance. Not enough time. First thing in the morning, my brother or one of his people will escort you and Darik out past the city limits as far as you want protection, maybe out to the ranch where Darik used to work. I'll put enough provisions in the wagon for you to get to New Mexico without starving to death. I'll toss in some extra clothes, blankets, and a couple of pistols and ammunition just in case. You and Darik need to go by Mrs. Brown's place by Bear Creek first thing in the morning to get your niece. The three of you need to get out of here for good, or at least until Riley's gone, and who knows, maybe someone'll figure out who he takes orders from and force that son of a bitch to also leave."

"Yes, we will go to Mrs. Brown's home," she said. "Mei Ling will never be safe here. She does not know Riley is her father, and it is my duty to make sure she never does. Riley hates her. He would kill her without a second thought because of his anger at me and hatred for all Chinese, even his own daughter. We will leave. Maybe you need to leave too."

"I'm a big boy," he said with a slight laugh. "A little flesh wound isn't much to worry about. I know how to protect myself.

With Nathan still having influence over a few folks in the police department, Riley'd have to be crazy to want to deal with me again. Just a hunch, of course, but since nobody lives forever, I want to make sure I continue to live the rest of my life by my own rules. I'll never allow some son of a bitch like Riley to control me or anyone I care about. I should have put a stop to him long ago."

Pere remounted the horse. With his hand extended, he lifted Lihua to a position behind him on the saddle. He nudged the horse with a couple of light taps, and they made their way back to his store within fifteen minutes, entering through the back door to avoid being seen.

He led Lihua into a large windowless pantry adjacent to his office and brought her an assortment of clothes he thought would be more suitable for traveling than her dress and torn blouse.

Pere sent the young errand boy at the livery over to the mill where Darik worked. It took less than an hour, roundtrip, for Darik and the boy to reach the rear entrance of the store. Darik tied off his horse just as Pere handed the boy a silver dollar and told him not to come back for a few days.

Adjacent to the mercantile, in a small barn where Pere stored supplies, the downsized Conestoga wagon he was giving to Darik and Lihua was next to the stall of one of Pere's strongest and healthiest horses. Pere completed loading the wagon with enough supplies to last at least two weeks, the length of time he estimated it would take Darik to reach Tejada.

"What's going on? What's the rush?" Darik asked as soon as he arrived. "Where's Lihua? Is she safe?"

"She's in the pantry putting on some traveling clothes for your ride to Tejada."

"What ride? Tejada? What's going on? No bullshit, Foster, what the hell's happening?"

"Riley's on to you and Lihua. Bastard ain't stupid. Nobody's ever accused him of that. Lihua was followed to the cemetery. Riley was alerted, rode out, and saw you kiss her. He arrived seconds after you rode away, so it's safe to say you messed up his plans by leaving when you did. He went to the cemetery to kill you and the girl; there's no doubt about it. He was so pissed you'd left that he used his horse to knock Lihua to the ground and then began smacking her around with a whip.

"Is she hurt?"

"Not much. Tore up her blouse, but scared the daylights out of her. She's fine. Tough gal. I got into it with Riley when I reached the cemetery so he didn't have time to do what he planned, which was to stomp your young lady to death."

"How'd you know to go there? Who told you?"

"My brother saw you at the cemetery. He's the big guy, the deputy marshal you've seen around here a few times. Pure coincidence he was at the cemetery when you got there. Nathan knew I'd take care of things myself, but l let my guard down after I had Riley on the ground. He fired his derringer, and that little piss ant bullet caught me on the edge of my shoulder. He's a lousy shot. Just a small flesh wound, but I shot him in the leg. I could have shot him in the belly and let him bleed to death, but making him walk home while bleeding after his horse ran off, that seemed like a better idea. I don't want to be accused of murder. Self-defense is on my side if he doesn't make it through the night."

Darik was stunned all this had happened after he left the cemetery.

"He's not just angry; he's a jealous man who's crazier than hell. Maybe things will change here in Denver eventually, but it's time for you two to move on. Best place for that is with your daughter.

Riley won't bother you in New Mexico. Too far. And I'm guessing he's got no leverage with anyone down there. He's not going to be happy, and I'm going to have to watch my own back even more than usual, but Nathan says it's likely Riley won't be doing much more business in Denver if a few of the more righteous citizens in town get their way, especially if we figure out who actually owns Riley. Even that jackass Bonfils, one of the owners of the *Denver Post,* is working with a federal marshal Nathan knows to try and find someone around here who's not being bribed by Riley and put a stop to him. I'd have you leave right now for New Mexico if I could, but it'll be nightfall in another hour. Last thing I want is for you to be traveling in the dark, even to Mrs. Brown's place," Pere added.

Darik walked into the storeroom where Lihua had been going through the women's work clothes Pere provided for the long ride to Tejada. She dropped a blouse to the ground when she saw Darik, ran to his open arms and embraced him.

"We are leaving Denver," she said. "In the morning we will get Mei Ling and take her with us to the place where your daughter lives. We will make a home there, or we will go someplace else if we have to so we can be together as a family."

He kissed her forehead. "Not exactly a fairy tale ending, is it? We're behaving like criminals on the run even though we haven't done anything wrong. We're leaving and Riley's staying. Doesn't make a lot of sense. Doesn't add up."

"Your daughter needs you. I need you. And Mei Ling needs us both. This makes sense."

Darik figured that the buckboard ride to Mrs. Brown's house would take nearly two hours. If he and Lihua left Pere's place by sunrise, they would arrive before nine, get Mei Ling, and then follow the Kit Carson Trail adjacent to the South Platte River for another hour or two, which would allow them to stay overnight at Eagle Trail Ranch. He was certain Mulroony and Silvano would provide protection. He thought he might ask if one of the ranch hands could ride alongside for added protection the next morning until they were far south of Denver.

"You look like a man on a mission," Pere said to Darik. "Let's double-check the wagon. It's my wedding gift to you, so no arguing about it. I've got others in as good a shape. Won't miss this one at all. The horse? Well, that's for being my friend. But I'm not selling the special birdhouse. You gotta take it with you."

"Will Riley come after you once we leave?" Darik asked in a serious tone.

"Maybe, but hopefully not until you're miles away. That bastard's got a lot of pull. Nathan's enlisted a couple of friends to stand guard outside the store overnight to make sure nothing goes wrong."

"Good idea," Darik replied.

"It's always a numbers game with Riley. Nothing's ever fair in his world. Hopefully we won't be bothered by them tonight. But who knows?"

Darik shrugged. "Lots could go wrong, so let's just make sure Lihua's safe."

"That's for sure. Listen, there's extra bedrooms upstairs above the shop. Pick one for tonight. You'll need some shut eye before heading out. What's the name of your village?"

"Tejada. Little place. Not on any maps. Just a tiny village twenty-five miles south of the Colorado border. It's at the base of the first set of foothills on the edge of the San Juans, maybe ten or twelve days ride in the wagon if the weather holds. Not quite two hundred miles. No trains go anywhere near it. The Wells

Fargo stage used to stop there, but they quit coming a couple years after I moved there. It's not as big as Fort Garland, where the regional trading post's located, or the size of Costilla, the first decent sized town across the New Mexico border to the west of the main trail over toward Alamosa. But that's only if I was going to head west and go through La Veta, and I don't want to deal with those mountains. The weather over there's hard to predict, and, hell, I don't need to go that far out of the way to be safe. We'll head due south. We can make twenty miles a day without pushing the horse. I'll ride alongside to keep the wagon lighter. Don't know if Lihua can drive a buckboard, but if not I'll teach her on the way to Mrs. Brown's. From Eagle Trail heading south, there's decent wagon trails all the way to Pueblo."

"Sounds like you're ready to go. Be sure to grab your birdhouse. Not like it's a jinx, but I don't need anyone asking questions about it after you've gone."

Darik took a quick inventory of the supplies Pere stowed in the wagon, including a thin rolled-up mattress pad large enough for Lihua and Mei Ling to use on the ground since the wagon's cargo bin was too full for anyone to sleep in it.

Pere also packed several large pieces of canvas bordered with grommets to attach to the side of the wagon to serve as a lien to. Two eight-gallon oak water barrels, each weighing eighty pounds when full, were attached to the sides of the wagon. Fresh water for the horses would be easily accessed during the ride since they would be following the South Platte and various small tributary streams. Despite the suddenness of the trip, everything was accounted for except Darik's carving tools which were at the rooming house near Union Station, less than a ten-minute horseback ride from Pere's store. Although he had some concern about heading back in that direction, he grabbed his hat and walked out the back door.

"Whoa. Where you headed?" Pere asked.

"Need to get my tools and some clothes at the rooming house. Won't take me but a few minutes. I can't replace those tools. I need them. I'll be fine. Right back."

Before either Pere or Lihua could say another word, Darik mounted his horse and headed to the rooming house from which he returned safely in less than an hour.

CHAPTER 26
Forthcoming

The kerosene lanterns on the second floor of the building were partially dimmed by the time supper was served. The main floor of the building was darkened. Darik, Lihua, Pere and Nathan, who had decided he would stay inside the store overnight for added security, quietly ate chicken stew and freshly baked soda bread brought over from the cafe next door. The cafe's owner, a German woman who was Pere's favorite tenant, knew nothing about the dangerous situation involving Riley, a man she also despised because of his foul temperament. She was pleased to prepare a meal for four people, especially since her landlord, Foster Pere, frequently ate his meals alone in her cafe.

"Stack up the dirty stuff," Pere said. "I'll take care of it in the morning. It's time you turn in."

He looked at Darik and Lihua. "You need to be on the trail no later than six. I'll be awake for a while doing paperwork downstairs."

"Keeping a loaded gun nearby?" his younger brother asked.

"Store's full of guns and ammunition. I'm not worried."

"They're all unloaded except that fancy Colt of yours, big brother, so maybe load up a shotgun and another pistol. Keep them within reach tonight."

"We think a lot alike. Get some sleep, Nathan. I'll wake you in a couple hours and we'll swap places. Deal?" Pere replied.

Nathan nodded, patted Foster lovingly on the back, and went into one of the bedrooms where he fell asleep in a matter of seconds. Lihua and Darik had left the dining table a few minutes earlier and were already sleeping, unaware that Foster Pere would be standing guard for the first few hours of the night.

Soaring high above the river basin as though he was once again the white falcon that so often guided him through his dreams, he was awestruck by the white-capped mountains, lush velvety fields of alfalfa, and endless acres of sunflowers covering the ground below. An eerie silence absorbed all the sounds of the wind and of nature itself while creating a setting reminiscent of a still-life painting. The bird swooped downward at a severe angle, its left wing nearly perpendicular to the ground, as flickering, bright orange and red flashing colors could be seen through the wispy clouds beneath his flight path. The pungent smell of burning wood and horse flesh, much like the fragrance of his encounter with the lightning five years earlier, became stronger as smoke began filling the falcon's eyes, burning as though acid was being poured into them. Shouting voices could be heard echoing in the sky, and then the falcon saw the pine and cottonwood forest below engulfed in flames that reached a hundred feet into the air. Before the bird of prey was able to change its course, it flew directly into the flames that somehow felt cold, almost like ice, as the bird's feathers became singed by the heat. On the far side of the flames stood Lihua, Mei Ling, and Darik's parents.

CHAPTER 27
Culmination

The sound of gunfire and shattering glass crashing to the floor blended with choking smoke to awaken Darik, Lihua and Nathan, each of whom slept fully dressed. All three sprang up. Nathan instinctively re-holstered his pistol and ran into the main hallway of the second floor where he heard gun shots being fired as his brother shouted for help. He bolted down the stairs.

Darik immediately sensed that the chaos beneath him was a direct threat to Lihua and pushed her back into the room.

"Don't move an inch. Stay put! If the smoke gets any worse, climb through the window and get on the ledge and climb down to the ground fast as you can. I'll be fine," he said although he had his doubts. Seeping through the sense of joy he had experienced since he and Lihua reunited, something had changed inside him, and he was only beginning to understand the profound responsibility he now felt for those whose lives were affected by his mere presence in Denver.

Lihua slammed the bedroom door and moved next to the window. She saw people scurrying around the front of the building with water buckets in hand. A fire wagon pulled up just as three men, volunteer firemen, began directing the others at a frenzied pace.

An exchange of gun shots rang out in the store as the burning building began shaking in response to the echoing explosions of ammunition in the cabinet and large glass-topped display cases. Shelving throughout the store collapsed to the floor. The voices below Lihua's room were so jumbled that it was impossible for her to differentiate them from one another, but it was obvious that Riley's people had attacked Foster Pere and were burning down the store.

By the time Darik reached the main floor, flames had engulfed the front entrance. The front door and large display window had been destroyed, and the interior was ablaze as the two Pere brothers, under siege, engaged in hand-to-hand combat with three assailants, one of whom Darik recognized as O'Connor, Riley's bodyguard. Darik had been in numerous fist fights at the ranch over the years, but in truth he had never taken part in what was certain to be mortal combat.

"Watch your backside, Pere!" Darik shouted although there was no way the man could have heard him. He then kicked out the back of a display case containing handguns, grabbed one of the Colt .45s, opened a box of bullets, and loaded the chamber.

"Go to hell, you son of a bitch!" he screamed as he took aim and fired at O'Connor who looked up just as the bullet pierced the center of his forehead. Darik was crazed with anger and a kind of fear he had never experienced in his life. No thought process took place in his mind; everything he did was instinctive although he had never taken the life of another human until that moment. A wild, crazed warrior began emerging from deep within him.

Darik turned to his left, toward Foster Pere. His friend gripped a long hunting knife in one hand, waving it viciously as he lunged toward one of Riley's men, the blade covered in blood; Pere's pistol was no longer visible. Darik could see blood pouring out from the left side of Pere's chest below the shoulder that had been wounded earlier in the day by Riley. Darik caught his gaze for a moment, and a look passed between them that reflected the strength of their immutable bond, one that only a father and son could share as the significance of their love for one another reached a crescendo, a connection that had been established over recent weeks, something neither man had initially sought. Darik ached to put time in reverse or slow its progress at least and find some way through the skirmish to fight by Pere's side since he could see that his friend was seriously injured yet continued to fight with the fierceness of a true warrior committed to protecting his loved ones.

Darik looked down momentarily to the floor where Riley lay motionless, blood oozing from a massive gash across his chest, his innards visible. He was certain that Pere's knife had caused Riley's wound and that the man was dead.

Nathan had reloaded his pistol twice during the melee, eventually shooting one of the assailants in the back of the neck as the man attempted to flee through the burning entryway. The man fell to the ground, his wound visible for a few seconds until flames began incinerating him.

Darik had run out of bullets and had suddenly lost sight of Pere whom he assumed was across the room fighting in another part of the inferno. Despite the blackish cloud of smoke filling the store, he saw an intact box of ammunition on the floor a dozen feet away but realized he would not have enough time to reload his weapon. Instinctively grabbing a tall, thin coat rack behind the main counter, without hesitation he charged forward in full stride towards the man Nathan was fighting.

"Bastard son of a bitch!" he screamed as the battle raged on. Nathan saw Darik's charge and felt an increased burst of adrenaline. Darik plunged the coat rack's brass-tipped cap into the assailant's neck as orange and blue flames spread out of control across the ceiling with the speed of wildfire.

Nathan turned to his side, shock overtaking him as he saw his older brother, Foster Pere, lying mortally wounded on the floor.

Darik had not seen his friend again before he bolted up the stairs, kicked in the bedroom door, grabbed Lihua by the hand, and rushed her out into the corridor.

"Go! Get out of here now! This fucking place is burning to the ground. Pere's supplies are fueling the fire, and the rest of the ammunition is bound to explode. Go!" he commanded. Even as he spoke, fleeting thoughts about the possibility of losing Lihua again flashed through his mind. There was nothing he would not do to protect her. In his own way, he prayed that she and his two friends would survive this battle even if he did not. His personal well-being seemed relatively unimportant at that moment as he was launched into manhood, fully, for the first time in his life. He had rediscovered his mate, but in the larger picture of things, her life had much more meaning than his own, and that was the case for Pere and Nathan.

Lihua ran down the stairs as fast as she could, sprinting toward the front entrance, making it through the flames without getting burned. She bolted past Nathan who was kneeling over a lifeless body whose face she did not recognize. When she reached the street, she was surrounded by dozens of onlookers who had gathered while volunteers tried in vain to extinguish the flames before the entire block of wooden framed businesses was destroyed. Even as she stood there with onlookers, she still failed to notice that the man Nathan was kneeling over was Foster Pere.

Darik used the blood-covered coat rack to smash open the display case containing Lihua's birdhouse. He grabbed it, ran toward the front door, and threw it with such force that when it struck a volunteer fireman in the chest, it knocked him to the ground. Lihua saw the birdhouse in flight, ran back closer toward the flaming building, picked it up, and carried it to safety. A portion of the roof was charred from the flames as an immense dark cloud of acrid smoke, fog-like, filled the air.

Once he saw Lihua across the street, Darik remained oblivious to who was safe and who was not, but he saw Nathan kneeling, tears rolling from his eyes. "Nathan, get the fuck out!" he yelled. "We're gonna burn! Whole place is going up in flames!"

Nathan stood slowly. In his arms was the outstretched body of his brother. Darik pushed him through what remained of the burning entrance, and they ran onto the street. Several volunteers doused them with water to keep their hair and clothes from burning. Darik then watched silently, in disbelief, as Nathan, now fifty feet from the front of the burning building, lowered the man's body to the ground.

As Darik recognized Foster Pere, dead, lying on the ground, the pounding of his heart suddenly underwent a colossal change as though everything in his world had come to a complete stop. He stood motionless as Nathan wailed uncontrollably. His concern about Lihua's safety was paramount throughout the battle, but in truth he had a sense that both Foster Pere and his brother, Nathan, were invulnerable, immune from death no matter what was taking place.

Who am I? he thought as shock consumed him. *Why am I alive? Why is he dead? Why does this keep happening? Why am I alive?*

Lihua, only a few feet away, watched the vacant expression on Darik's face take hold as his posture weakened, his knees wobbled, and he dropped to the ground. Lihua placed the birdhouse on the ground, hurried back to the dead man's body, kneeled down, placed a loving kiss on his cheek, and then wrapped her arms around Nathan before embracing Darik tightly in an attempt to ease his pain.

"It is not your fault, Darik," she whispered into his ear although she had no way of knowing if he heard her or could hear anything else taking place as the inferno reached its peak and the disharmonic sounds of chaos filled the air.

Three fire wagons arrived within minutes. Their crews joined forces with the forty men already fighting the blaze to prevent the flames from spreading to the businesses on the adjacent block south and to the Colorado State Bank's headquarters across the street.

The sounds of men shouting, fire alarm bells clanging, and the collapsing of buildings attached to Foster Pere's mercantile, including the cafe owned by the German woman, were, at this point, beyond Darik's conscious thoughts. His tears, salty and charred from the smoke, dripped down onto the body of his friend. After a lifetime of failing to confront his true feelings about the loss of his parents, his entire sense of being had become elevated when he and Lihua reconnected. Yet suddenly he imagined himself back on the rocky cliff in Sedona, hallucinating with Fierce Night Sky, viewing the fire that took his parents lives nearly thirty years earlier. He traveled back and forth between his childhood in Romania and the torment he was now experiencing from this disaster in Denver as he stared at Foster Pere's lifeless body. He felt catapulted into a powerful terror from which he knew he had to escape immediately as his mind raced erratically in multiple directions.

He looked up, wiped the tears from his eyes, and watched several men rapidly lead the horses and wagons out of the small barn behind Foster Pere's store before the barn was consumed in flames. One of Pere's wagons, the small Conestoga-style buckboard filled with supplies intended to be used by Darik and Lihua on their journey to Tejada, was pushed to safety. Even in a state of shock with random, irrational thoughts spilling from his mind, he was keenly aware that Foster Pere had given his own life in order to provide the means for him, Lihua, and Mei Ling to join Theresa and Lynetta in Tejada.

"He's given me my life. I have to prove I've earned it. He's given me my life," he concluded as a momentary sense of calm flowed through his body.

The entire block was destroyed by the fire. Nothing remained but blackened wooden beams, large piles of glowing embers, and bricks so charred that it was impossible to decipher their actual color. Reporters from *The Denver Post* and its rival publication, the *Rocky Mountain News,* had been on the scene since the gun battle ended and the fire burned itself out. They hounded the survivors and the police to learn the details of the assault led by Riley and his gang.

Darik and Lihua, both wrapped in blankets and sitting on the sidewalk on the far side of the street, refused to respond to any questions from the reporters as Nathan provided his own modified description of what had taken place, skipping any reference to Lihua and Darik's actual connection to Riley. He simply described the couple as friends of his now-deceased brother, one of the city's most respected businessmen, a civic leader who was murdered by one of the city's most reviled criminals.

Nathan was interviewed by a detective, a friend of his, and underwent questioning from the fire chief and the city's unpopular and corrupt mayor. Within two days after the fire, as incriminating evidence was gathered and the public became fully aware of what had been taking place, both newspapers speculated the mayor would be fired and possibly arrested. Riley's criminal activities and the corruption in Denver government finally got front page visibility. The publishers of both newspapers had never allowed the entire truth to be reported previously because of their own backroom relationships with Riley and others of his ilk.

After the commotion lessened, one of Nathan's colleagues took Darik and Lihua to Nathan's home. They bathed, changed into borrowed nightclothes, and slept like babies until eleven that morning.

A series of brief nightmarish scenes pummeled Darik throughout the night. Unlike the mystical dreams he had experienced throughout his life, the nightmares caused him to have uncontrollable chills as he soaked his portion of the bed with sweat. The only saving grace, the only means for him to escape the night terrors, was to place his hand on Lihua's shoulder as she slept.

The investigation continued for two days. Darik and Lihua stayed in Nathan's home to avoid any contact with reporters. The terror finally subsided, yet the loss of his best friend continued to cause Darik to feel as though the ground had collapsed beneath him. Even while Lihua held him tightly multiple times over those days, he grieved openly for the first time in his life, repeatedly crying uncontrollably. His facial expression appeared glazed as he seemed to stare aimlessly into his thoughts.

Lihua, for different reasons, felt the tragic loss just as powerfully. They exchanged few words during those first days after the fire, simply hugging, kissing, and walking hand in hand through Nathan's yard to assure one another that they would never allow themselves to be separated again.

Foster Pere's funeral was held at week's end at the same cemetery where Riley had accosted Lihua a few days earlier when Pere had come to her rescue, although that information was never made public. *The Denver Post* reported that more than three hundred Denverites as well as a number of ranchers and farmers from the surrounding area, including Mulroony and Silvano, attended the burial.

Two days after the funeral, with the investigation complete, crews began cleaning up the site of the massive fire. Six buildings had been destroyed, all of which were owned and built by Foster Pere over the prior decade as he had done all he could do to help Denver, the state capital, grow into its role as a center for regional commerce. The clean-up and salvage work took another week.

Once completed, all that remained was a flat, barren piece of land measuring one acre located right in the center of Denver's most vibrant business district. Nathan, a silent partner in all of his late brother's business and real estate ventures, including co-ownership of the mercantile, resigned from his job as a deputy marshal. Numerous offers to purchase the entire block began soon thereafter, but Nathan declined them all, including top-dollar propositions, indicating that it would be several months before he and his wife would make any decisions.

Mrs. Brown came to the city, temporarily leaving her summer home adjacent to the sunflower field where Lihua and Darik had first met more than five years earlier, and she again took up residence in her spacious greystone mansion located walking distance from Riley's now deserted home. At the direction of Nathan Pere, who had ridden out to Mrs. Brown's country property the day after his brother had died, she brought Mei Ling with her so the child could reunite with her Aunt Lihua. Mrs. Brown never exchanged words with Nathan nor said goodbye to Mei Ling, nor did she express interest in speaking to Lihua nor Darik when she handed over Mei Ling to Nathan.

Riley, a criminal for whom no one in Denver shed a tear, was buried in an unmarked grave at the city cemetery, a funeral that only Mrs. Brown and two grave diggers attended.

Nathan had heard rumors over the years that Mrs. Brown had been the primary source of funds for the businesses Riley operated, some even believing that she was Riley's employer. Both newspapers avoided mentioning her name in subsequent articles relating to Riley and the tragic events in downtown Denver. However, several reporters believed that following her earlier career as a prostitute in Leadville years prior to becoming a member of Denver's high society, she had applied her working knowledge of brothels and bars to the operation of several unsavory local businesses that Riley was thought to have owned.

The reunion of the young girl with her Aunt Lihua was joyful as was her surprise when she was re-introduced to Darik as the man who would become her father after they completed their move from Denver to the village of Tejada, New Mexico, where her new sister, Theresa, would be waiting.

Twenty days after the fire, a small Conestoga-style wagon drawn by one horse and driven by Darik Jacoby, his horse tied to the side of the wagon, headed south from Denver to Eagle Trail Ranch with an escort provided by Nathan Pere, his wife, and a few other well-wishers.

THE END

Author Bio

Hank Fisher traces his Colorado roots to the arrival of his Russian great-grandparents in America, where they eventually helped establish the Colorado settlement of Montrose on the state's Western Slope just prior to the town's legal formation in 1882. His family's Colorado legacy is directly linked to the agriculture industry as farmers, ranchers, stockyards management, and meat packing—the industry in which Hank grew up and later worked with his father and brother as co-owners of a successful Denver-based packing house.

Hank has explored a variety of writing genres, including business journalism, marketing and advertising, strategic brand development, essays, poetry, lyrics, and fiction. This exposure to multiple styles has helped shape his love for storytelling and fuels the colorful, highly descriptive narratives incorporating urban and nature-based metaphors and symbolism intertwined in his writing.

Hank earned his degree in Sociology at the University of Colorado where he specialized in Collective Behavior and Inter-Group Relations, which led to in-depth studies about the development and behavior of cults. He credits the cultivation of his serious love for wordplay during his college years to a class in Greek Mythology in 1969 taught by the renowned mythologist Hazel Barnes; a poetry workshop taught by celebrated poet Reginald Saner; and a solid year in a fiction writing workshop under the tutelage of noted author Jose Antonio Villarreal.

Hank is the proud father of two adult children, David and Rachel. He currently resides walking distance from Bear Creek, a few miles east of the foothills, with the love of his life, the internationally acclaimed author and storyteller, Dr. Anita Johnston.

The author can be reached at fisherh@comcast.net.